To Phy.

CW00544007

MISUNDERSTANDINGS

Maggi Wales

Maggi Wales
(aka Valeri Francis)

Published in 2022 by FeedARead.com Publishing

A CIP catalogue record for this title is available from the British Library.

Cover photograph: stanley45

Prologue

"Come on girl, you're late, her father tousled her hair."
Morien opened her eyes sleepily.

"What's up? Why so early?

"I want to put Merlin through his paces now before the
daily razzmatazz gets under way. He's nearly ready to join the
other horses, perhaps tonight's show."

"Good idea. I'll see you later."

Morien luxuriated in the special extra minutes. Not for
long though as there were horses to feed. She washed, dressed
and grabbed a couple of biscuits. Standing outside the caravan
having a much-needed stretch she heard a commotion across the
site. She ran to investigate and, to her horror, saw that one of
the circus lions had escaped and the handlers were trying to
corner it.

"Chase it toward the Big Top," shouted one of the men.
"It'll be easier to get him in an enclosed space. I'll round him up
from this side."

"No, no," yelled Morien running towards the tent.
"Dad's in there with Merlin."

"Christ," was the response. But it was too late. Their
corralling had worked. The lion entered the Big Top at a run.
Morien rushed through the opening in time to see Merlin rear up
and twist with panic flinging her father against the temporary
seating and then gallop for the exit almost knocking Morien over
as he passed.

With no thought for the lion, Morien rushed into the tent
to her father who lay inert in the sawdust like a crumpled doll.
On her knees, Morien cradled him in her arm, trying to stem the
flow of blood from his head. There was no response.

"Dad, Dad," she whispered sobbing. "Dad, come back
to me." Frantically she massaged around his heart, hoping for a
slight flutter. She found no response.

Meanwhile the lion was captured and many of the circus
artists crowded in surrounding Morien and Pavo. Renaldo, the
clown, leaned down and felt for a pulse With a sigh he caressed
Morien's hair.

"Come, little one," he said gently. "It's over."

CHAPTER 1

Two weeks later.

Absolute devastation. Her father really was dead, this charismatic vibrant man who had filled every moment of her life, whose energy still floated in the caravan with the expectancy of his suddenly appearing through the door? She sat at the table, almost afraid to look up. Her father and his circus horses were her whole world and with a single stroke it had disintegrated.

But it was true. The grief of her loss was still so strong. So suddenly she was on her own. Somehow she had managed to continue the act each evening with a few modifications and, like an automaton had continued the everyday tasks and the regular travelling of the circus. But all the everyday things gave her pain because her father wasn't there as usual to share them. Morien had nightmares of body snatchers and the stabling going up in flames, threatening her and the horses. The numbness since the accident was beginning to wear off as reality made itself felt. Her thoughts raced back to that terrible day. It was a mercy death had been instantaneous. Her mind shuddered away.

She hadn't realised her meagre savings were so small until she went to the undertakers. She only had her "pocket money" for the work she did. There wasn't much, representing a lifestyle to date. She knew nothing of her father's finances. He'd always provided for what little they needed. He'd been such a private man and she, being used to her sheltered life, had never questioned or even thought about such things.

These recollections brought another wave of misery over her and with it the image of the gentle lady at the undertakers who explained

"The cheapest option in the circumstances is the basic funeral." Tears had welled in Morien's eyes. "I know it's hard but other ways are expensive," she had said. "We would have the cremation early in the day. There can be no mourners or family."

Morien gulped back her sobs. She knew a cremation was the only way, but not to be there, to be with him in those last hours, that was the ultimate blow.

"Do I get the ashes?" she had whispered.

"Yes, of course, dear. They will be available the following morning."

"Thank you."

"If you want us to handle this for you, I'm afraid we will need a deposit and all the details."

In a haze Morien had filled in all the forms and handed over the money. What choice had she had?

The memory brought more tears. Morien buried her face in her hands trying to stem the flow, when the trailer door suddenly opened and Gino Trento, the ringmaster, stepped inside unannounced. Without looking up she knew it was him. His whole personality seemed to radiate heat with the smell of garlic.

"Well, there's a pretty sight." He came up close behind her.

"Why are you slacking? There's work to be done. Waiting for me?" He thrust a plastic jar on the table.

"Your father's ashes," he said. Morien drew back in shock, repulsed Coming from Gino had somehow contaminated the urn.

"What, no thank you or a hug?" Gino smirked as Morien shrank further into a corner. "And there I was doing you a favour."

"Thank you," she whispered.

"Well, now there are some things we need to get straight," said Gino. "Your father owns nothing. He arrived one night when we were travelling in Europe with four horses destitute and you in a papoose on his back, a refugee from some local war, so he said, begging for help. So many refugees all asking for help. Your father had the edge though – four attractive looking horses.

I made a deal with him, agreed the circus would employ and provide for him as long as his act was popular."

"So at least he brought horses when he came," exclaimed Morien.

"That was a long, long time ago. Said he had property and would pay me back. In truth, he was penniless. But that's just water under the bridge now."

"That's not fair."

"Why not? You've had a good livelihood all these years, haven't you?"

There was little Morien could say as she didn't know the facts.

"When we get the new act, I'll be needing the mares. You can keep the stallion. He's no use to me."

Morien was dumbstruck. Her father's precious horses in the hands of who knew who? But then a level of relief flooded over her about Merlin, which she kept hidden as she wriggled out of the corner to find a home for the urn, indicating that there was nothing more to say.

Gino stepped up behind her, sliding an insinuating arm around her waist.

"No time like the present." It was clear he had no intention of letting her go.

Morien tried to fight him off, but he pushed her backwards onto the trailer bench.

"No, no," she gasped as, shifting slightly, Gino wrenched at the belt holding her jeans.

"Come on my little tiger, playing hard to get. Don't waste your time," his fevered eyes showed his pleasure as he deliberately bit her lip.

"Gino to the microphone van. Gino to the microphone van." The circus public address system blasted into the caravan. Gino raised his head and cursed. Then turned again to subduing Morien who was still struggling.

"Gino urgently needed at the microphone van. Gino urgently needed at the microphone van." Again, the tannoy interrupted. Reluctantly, he shoved her away.

"Saved by the bell," he jeered. "Never mind, anticipation is part of the fun. You'll not escape." Morien regarded him in horror.

"What do you mean? she whispered.

"I'm afraid this trailer isn't yours either. I lent your father the money for it as well as all the subsequent horses and he never paid me back. The new act will need it." Gino reached towards her again. Morien turned away to hide her dismay.

"Get away from me."

"You can come in with me, my dear," he said sensuously fondling her breast. Morien pulled away, flicking back her golden hair, her eyes, bright green from her tears, flashing angrily.

"How can you say that to me? You're a monster."

"What, when I am offering you a lifeline - staying with me?"

7

"Yes, you'd like that wouldn't you? What did you have in mind – a nightly rape?"

"How ungrateful you are."

"You've taken Father's horses and then you spring these unexpected debts on me when my pockets are totally empty."

"Not all, my dear, you've still got Merlin. and me" Gino pulled her hard against him, ignoring her struggles.

"Nobody wants Merlin because he's too young and now has a reputation, so I wouldn't even have an act - just the Ringmaster's mistress." As she fought against him suddenly Gino thrust her brutally away causing her to fall. The tannoy calling Gino rang out again.

"Well, take it or leave it. You're as stand-offish as your father with all your airs and graces. You've got till the new act arrives. I'm certainly not accommodating hangers on." The circus chief smirked

"Oh and, by the way, I want you to put all new applicants through their paces, so we get a good act." He turned about and left, slamming the door. Morien was dumbstruck. Was she not going to be part of the act now? Apparently not.

Morien scrambled to her feet, glad she hadn't said something she might regret, she eyed the closed door and let her gaze wander around the familiar space that had been her home for as long as she could remember. Now it was soiled, smelled of his sweat and his threats. The proximity of the circus's evening performance had rescued her from his determined intention to rape her. She knew it was only a temporary respite on this occasion. Gino always got his way.

Sighing Morien gazed again at the plastic urn containing his ashes. Knowing she should be outside preparing for tonight's show, she climbed on the bunk, stretching for the high shelf above, pushing the urn towards the back.

Losing the horses was giving away a part of herself. Her father had bred them. They had known no other life but the circus since they were born. Merlin though had been labelled a killer and superstition had exiled him.

Despite having survived her ordeal Morien was more shocked than she realised. She had only been moments away from losing her virginity and to someone so disgusting and undesirable as Gino. Her father had naturally warned her about predators.

8

Circus life attracted many itinerants, here today and gone tomorrow. She had learned how to take care of herself and, of course, her father was always within reach. But in her present circumstances of worry and being dependent on Gino and the circus she had been taken unawares. Never again she vowed. The whole episode had been so repulsive.

Next week! Today was Tuesday. She had to get out of this contaminated space. Regardless of further unwanted intrusions, she flung open all the windows. After all what was there left for her now? She no longer had anything to do for the daily performances, except sell programmes. She headed for the horse lines.

She rubbed her bruised arms before starting gingerly to groom her precious Merlin. What did a girl with a valueless horse and no money do to stay alive? Merlin's training was insufficient for a single act, and she realised she knew pathetically little about the outside world. Her eyes were damp with tears. She was afraid.

Those awful moments kept thrusting into her mind as she tried to focus on her current untenable situation.

When she appeared at the horse lines all the horses came to the doors and knickered a greeting. "Hello my darlings," she said. "I have some news for you. Uncle Gino is going to look after you for now." Welling up she buried her face against the nearest mare's neck. She felt she was giving away a part of herself. She moved down the line caressing each animal, giving it a carrot treat.

When she reached Merlin's stable she went in and started grooming him. "I know you're missing Dad," she said, "but I want you to know it wasn't your fault. It was that horrible lion that gave you a fright. You're not a killer like everyone is saying."

Fear again took over in her mind. How could she keep Merlin when the whole circus was ostracising him? Her future looked bleak. Her stressful musing was interrupted.

"Morien." She turned to find the chief clown beside her, as the shadow of Renaldo's tall figure fell across the horse, his face showing his concern. "Come on now, brush away your tears. You're spoiling that pretty face."

"I know, I know." She sniffed "But I'm frightened. Gino's just been propositioning me - either his mistress for my keep or I go."

Renaldo frowned. "Trust him. He's been eyeing you for months. He looked at her more closely, seeing the swelling rising on her mouth. "Has he been hurting you?"

Morien turned away. She was so ashamed. She felt dirty and knew if it got out about Gino's attack, she would get the blame.

"Oh, it's nothing," she prevaricated. Renaldo didn't pursue his thought.

"Have you got any plans?"

"I don't know where to begin. If it was only me, I could try another circus, help with the horses, but would they take Merlin? I expect by now other circuses will have heard on the grapevine about the accident and Merlin's involvement so they will reject him too. And with Merlin in tow, who'd have me? It's two mouths to feed."

"Why don't you sell him? He's quite well bred and outside on the open market they don't have our superstitions."

"As what? I couldn't bear it, Renaldo. He might go for slaughter and he's all I have left." She stifled another sob.

Renaldo was quiet for a long time, deep in thought, as he gently caressed the horse. Morien thought he'd forgotten she was there and began to groom again, lost in her misery.

"I have an old friend," the clown interrupted her musing. "He owes me a favour which I've never taken up. He knew your dad too as he once worked this circus. He's got a place not far from here and I'm sure he keeps horses. I think there's a riding school or something." Morien's eyes shone. Was there a way out? Renaldo smiled. "I'll try to contact him and see if he'll take you on to help in the stables. Got to rush now to get ready for this evening."

Was there a chance to escape from Gino? If so, how would she cope? She was born to circus life and had no real knowledge of the "outside world". She hadn't needed to know. The circus travelled as a large family completely self-contained. They never stayed anywhere long enough to make connections, a few nights here, a few nights there. Always being on the move precluded any chance to have any permanent friends although she did go to school for a few months once or twice in the winter rest periods.

Her father had a fetish about education and standards of behaviour. She'd quite enjoyed that totally alien world of school, although it made her unpopular with the other circus families – stuck up, they'd muttered. Perhaps she'd be better off remaining with the circus after all. If Renaldo did find her a job with his friend, would she be up to it? Doubts rose within her. But as the vision of Gino's lascivious face rose in her mind, she knew she couldn't stay. She would have to take the plunge if it were offered to her.

Morien did everything possible to avoid Gino. She was in constant fear of further rape attempts. She kept her arms covered to hide the masses of blue and yellow bruises that had surfaced. She deliberately made sure she was in someone's company and never on her own during the day. After much searching through her father's effects, she had found the key, never used before and locked the door at night. Such precautions had never been necessary. She didn't get much sleep since she was constantly on the qui vivre. Every noise expanded in her imagination and the nightmares started up again of leaping horses, lions, dead bodies and strange things touching her in the dark.

The next days had an extra purgatory, with the prospective performers riding her precious horses. The first lot were so incompetent that one of them was bucked off, rolling round in the sawdust. The third lot were downright cruel, yanking at the horses' mouths and using spurs. Morien went to bed each night in tears after attending to all the horses' injuries.

Yesterday, at last, they found a nice family who seemed in tune with their mounts. Gino had employed them straight away as the circus had to move on. Morien was faced with an uncertain future.

She longed for word from Renaldo and time dragged. One minute she was excited planning her new life and the next in the depths of despair. With the yo-yo emotions, she found herself on the fringe. In a circus, everyone has a role and work to do. She felt like a spare part and knew the others were wary of her. She was aching for an answer – good or bad.

After seemingly endless days, Morien climbed the steps of Renaldo's trailer. She sat down abruptly as his nod and smile ended her suspense. "Yes, they'll take you. It's a riding school run for my friend by his son, who is away on a lecture tour at present."

"He's truly got space for Merlin too?"

"Yes. He's quite excited about having you and the horse. I met him many years ago when he and his wife had a high wire act. We all worked the circus together. Sadly, one night the wire snapped, and Alison was killed. You may remember, although you were very young. Nathan broke his back and is now confined to a wheelchair. He depended on me for quite some time. He understands sorrow too, Morien." Renaldo gave her a quick hug.

"That's really sad when we always take such care with equipment especially as our lives often depend on it."

"True, but it's a risk we often take, not only for the audience but also for the thrills we get. Anyway, Nathan says they take in horses for schooling and train students too. I remember from when I took him back after his injury it's a biggish farm, arable farming and stock rearing. But Nathan only seemed connected to the smaller buildings in the stable area."

"That's relief. Don't think I'm up to farming." Morien laughed.

"Nathan remembers you and Pavo. He says you're to work with the horses. Grooming them etc. for the riders I expect. They will provide you with a room and stabling for Merlin. You will get your keep and Merlin's food and probably a little pocket money."

"It sounds too good to be true. How soon can I go?"

"When I told Nathan of your dilemma, he said to send you straight away," smiled Renaldo

"What all the gruesome details?"

"An edited version but indicating urgency. After all he knew Gino from the past."

"Oh, thanks so much. Is this place far from here?"

"No, not far. It's called Wilton Hall. We'll have to work out how to get you there."

"I'll ride," exclaimed Morien gleefully. "After all nothing much here belongs to me apart from a few clothes."

"Don't leave everything behind in the heat of the moment. Leave stuff with me. I can always send it on by road or rail once I know you're settled."

"Oh, thank you." Morien felt relieved.

12

"We are within a few miles so you could go tomorrow." Renaldo dug around in the cupboard for a map. "We don't want you arriving exhausted since you're there to work, not have a holiday." Together they worked out the route.

"I'm definitely going in the morning," said Morien. "Even a few more days with that creature stalking me will be too much."

Renaldo laughed. "He never realised he'd cut off his nose to spite his face. Silly man."

"There should be a health and safety warning for all the other girls." giggled Morien.

"Go to bed now and tell Gino in the morning you're fixed up. Oh and don't forget to bring me any stuff you can't carry. I'll keep it safe."

Back in the trailer Morien could hear all the familiar sounds of the temporary structures of the circus being dismantled for moving on. She should be out there helping, but somehow that no longer mattered. She'd decided to put Merlin in his travelling box so the others wouldn't guess she wasn't going with them. In the morning, she would simply unload him, tack up and ride away.

Her stomach fluttered. No time to muse. She began sorting out what she'd take with her. It's like dismantling my life, she thought. I seem to own so little – some books, her precious snowman, a few clothes. She looked at her spangles, hesitating, then flung them back in the drawer. What use were they now? Let the new act have them.

Then she hesitantly opened the drawer below her father's bunk feeling like an intruder. They both had always respected their personal spaces. To her surprise there was a suit, a sort of military uniform or perhaps local costume. She had never seen it before. Lifting it out carefully she placed it on the bed. Below she found a photo album and a bulky envelope which seemed to hold lots of papers, all in a foreign language. Below these in one corner was a pair of gold cufflinks with a strange inscription. She was hit by the fact now her father had gone and there was so little of him to show he ever existed.

One by one she put all the bits and pieces into a box for Renaldo, stopping a moment to caress her father's treasured photo album. Nostalgia threatened. She'd never spent much time looking at the photos and her father hadn't encouraged her.

13

He'd rarely brought it out. It seemed sort of private. She's assumed the faded pictures were of his earlier life. There wasn't time to look now so she shoved it in with the other items, placing the suit on top ready to leave with Renaldo.

She decided to brave telling Gino straight away and went in search of him. She'd chosen a moment when there were others there to witness. What a pleasure it was. Gino's chagrin was written all over him.

"Gino, I've just come to tell you I've found another job and so I won't be needing the accommodation you offered."

"What's all this?"

"You heard. I have another job and Merlin and I will be leaving in the morning." Morien backed away as Gino made a move towards her. Then he thought better of it when he noticed the others watching.

"Well good luck to you then. I'm not offering any references." He stamped off in high dudgeon.

After only a few hours of sleep, in the bleak light of dawn, Morien picked up her loaded rucksack, cast a final look at her "life" and went to fetch Merlin.

"You'll have to manage without breakfast," she whispered, tacking him up. With one last look, she mounted and rode out the gate. It was all over, tomorrow had come.

CHAPTER 2

So here she was. Wilton Hall - Morien looked in utter amazement as she rode up to the elegant wrought iron gates with their impressive message. Renaldo certainly hadn't really prepared her for something quite so grand. On one of the pillars was an engraved brass plaque with the words 'Classical Riding Establishment'.

"Merlin," she said, patting his neck. "What have we let ourselves in for?" The picture she had had in her mind was of a sort of rustic farm with stables - a riding school belonging to his old circus pal, she thought Renaldo had said.

Merlin tossed his head and pawed the ground impatiently. He looked magnificent as his flowing mane was caught by the light breeze. He was a well-muscled stallion approaching sixteen hands – dappled with large, darkened rings on his grey coat. Morien sat the horse well, her slim bronzed body held gracefully erect gave her an aristocratic air despite her jeans and wind-blown honey hair.

Peering through the gates she could see a wide drive sweeping through open parkland studded with oak trees. The gates were imposing, with crests emblazoned into the wrought iron and the supporting pillars were topped with stone lions glaring down at her. They were set into a flint stone wall which stretched away on both sides.

She hesitated. Could this be the place? There must be some mistake. Surely a retired circus pal wouldn't be able to afford a place as large as this. Perhaps there was a hack hire in the vicinity.

She decided to ride a little further down the road to see if there was another stable yard with a similar name, but there was nothing but the endless wall on one side and fields on the other So, she had no choice. As nostalgia for the circus threatened to overwhelm her, a vision of Gino crossed her mind re-iterating those fateful words that had transformed her life.

Controlling her rising panic, she rode through the gates. It was obviously a very large place. There were actual signposts indicating the direction to its various occupations - Home Farm, Main House, Greenhouses, Stables. Morien could now see the

Main House with its magnificent Corinthian columns at the front door. It was huge and must have masses of bedrooms. It reminded her of a National Trust house she had visited as a child. She remembered Renaldo had said his friend lived in the stable area, so she followed the signs to the Stables and came upon an elegant flint stone wall broken by a huge arch, topped with a clock and weathervane.

Dismounting, she led Merlin through into the square yard with loose boxes on three sides. Horses gazed contentedly over the stable doors at central lawns cascading with flowers. It was so clean and tidy; it didn't look real. Doves cooed from the roofs. Morien was absorbing the peace of the place when an immaculately turned-out young lady appeared, looking her up and down speculatively.

"You must be Morien Castini. We are expecting you and your horse." She frowned at her. "Do you usually ride without a hat?"

"Oh, er yes, er no." Morien muddled her identity with her lack of hat, feeling decidedly scruffy in her jeans and tousled hair "I mean, yes, I'm Morien," she finished lamely offering a very grubby hand.

"My name is Helen," said the paragon ignoring the hand. "I'm the Head Girl here." Then somewhat kindlier "Are you on your own? Only a rucksack, no other gear or anything?" Morien nodded. Helen seemed rather surprised but did not comment further. "Come, let's put the horse away and get you settled in."

Helen led the way, passing numerous ancillary stable blocks. "That was the main yard we've just left. The one over there on the right is the garden block." Helen walked on briskly.

Then they passed an outside row of stalls where rather scruffy ponies were tethered. Seeing Morien gazing at them in surprise Helen said: "These animals are used for our disabled riders. They are very gentle and seem to understand the pleasure they are giving. I've put your horse down here in the old block nearest to the paddock."

At the furthest end of the block a stable door opened to emit a slim girl with untidy dark curls. She was about the same age as Morien but shorter and plumper. She gave Morien a happy grin, pushing up her shirtsleeves to reveal brown muscular arms.

"Ah, Gill."

16

"Helen," she exclaimed "I've just finished."

"The day you start doing things on time will be a red-letter day for me," said Helen shortly. "This is Morien. Bring her to my office after you've settled the horse." Helen smiled and left.

"Stuck up so and so," muttered Gill after Helen's retreating back.

"She is a bit frightening," commented Morien.

Gill turned her attention to the horse. "Bring him in. Isn't he beautiful?" she said gazing at him adoringly. "How old is he?"

"He's just 5. I've had him since he foaled. My father bred him."

"What's his name?"

"Merlin."

"How romantic," sighed Gill. "I read all the books I can get hold of about Merlin and Arthur and all his knights. He's just the sort of horse Merlin would ride." Morien smiled

"Well, he's not into magic …. Yet."

"Did you name him?

"Oh no. My father was always on the lookout for good stock in his travels. He took his favourite mare to a special stallion, I can't remember, somewhere near Glastonbury, hence the name."

"Sounds quite a pedigree."

"Well, he certainly knows how to move through his paces."

"That should make him popular here," said Gill "That's all they ever seem to talk about. 'Oh, what a lovely movement. Ah, look at that action. Comes through nicely from behind.'" Gill mimicked, much to Morien's amusement.

Gill gave the horse a pat and began to rub him down while Morien removed the saddle and bridle and slung them over her arm, hitching up her backpack. Merlin, having taken everything in, began to munch contentedly at the hay net.

"Hey, no one said he was a stallion," exclaimed Gill who had been giving him a final check over. Morien looked aghast.

"Does that matter? I'm so used to him I never gave it a thought. He's got perfect manners," she said proudly.

"Well, Helen may want to re-stable him. Here by the paddocks, he will get wind of the stud mares. Speaking of her, we'd better hurry."

Morien felt apprehensive as they made their way to one of the other blocks. The place seemed like an unending maze, and she

17

was sure she would soon have got lost on her own. Gill quickly showed her the tack room to stow her saddle and bridle. There were rows and rows of them, and she only hoped she would be able to find it again. They briefly discussed Merlin's food, adding his name to the feeding charts.

"Does he really survive on just hay and so few oats?" enquired Gill

"He seems lively and fit enough," returned Morien "Neither my father nor I believe in man-made mixtures. We like to know exactly what is going in."

"Well, I suppose you don't want a stallion to be too much above himself," acknowledged Gill as they headed for Helen's office.

"I'll leave you here," said Gill. She noticed Morien's nervousness. "Helen's all right really. She has to be bossy to keep us all in order, so don't be afraid." Morien tapped on the door and went in.

"Sit down, Morien and tell me something about yourself." Morien hesitated. Where did she begin? She didn't want to mention the circus in this upmarket place. She'd have to make something up. She should have thought about a story in advance. She needed them to realise she knew about horses and could care for them. She was just about to speak when the telephone interrupted. "Head Girl speaking. Yes, she's here with me now." Helen listened with obvious surprise. "Yes . I'll settle her into her room and then send her up. About half an hour?" She turned to Morien "That was the Earl checking your arrival. He wants to see you."

Morien was dumbstruck. An Earl ? Where was Renaldo's friend, Nathan? This was getting worse and worse. Then she pulled herself together. This was an adventure, a new world. It was too late to retreat now. She straightened her shoulders.

They walked up the broad path to a small door in the side wing of the mansion. "You must realise," said Helen, "that to visit Sir Nathan is somewhat exceptional, but then so is your unexpected arrival. I understand you have a family connection." Morien nodded non-committaly as Helen continued "I would appreciate it if you didn't discuss these private matters with the other girls. It could lead to friction, and we haven't got time for that. You are here as a Working Pupil. Working Pupils are generally accepted to work in exchange for their keep and their tuition."

"I understand," murmured Morien still recovering from the discovery she was going to meet an Earl. Why hadn't Renaldo mentioned it? Probably thought he'd frighten me away.

"First, I'll show you your room so you can freshen up." Along the corridor at the top of the stairs, Helen opened the door on a small but bright and comfortable bed sitting room. "All the girls have rooms on this floor".

"What a pretty room," exclaimed Morien

"The bathroom's down the corridor, last door. You'll need to change. When you're ready, go down the stairs, through the oak door on your left into the main hallway where the butler, Rankin, will be waiting for you."

"Thanks a lot."

"I'll expect you in the yard at 6.30 a.m. to-morrow. Oh, and by the way, you'll find breakfast and your other meals downstairs to the left of the door we came in by." Helen disappeared.

Morien felt panicky. Everything was so alien and different from the circus where you simply take everything with you - the old, the familiar, no strange rooms or people, just the caravan and your family and friends.

The room was small and bright with bed, dressing table and chair and a small desk in one corner. She realised it was the first time she had ever slept in a room or even had one to herself. She hadn't thought this far ahead and felt quite silly to have been so short-sighted. She sat on the bed and bounced a little. Why hadn't Renaldo told her more? He must have realised how she'd feel. Courage, she thought. Now was not the time to speculate but to act. She'd better hurry.

She fished in her rucksack for a dress. It had a few creases, so she hung it up in the bathroom while she took a shower. The steam improved it just enough, so when she slipped it over her head the dress clung a little, emphasising her willowy figure and long legs She combed her hair, so it fell in a golden cap flattering her petite features. She never wore make-up out of the ring but decided to use some lipstick to bolster her flagging courage. After all a 'Sir' to her was almost royalty. At last, considerably cleaner and more presentable she made her way to the main part of the house, entering through a studded wooden door.

CHAPTER 3

The house was enormous, like entering a museum or a town hall. She was standing uncertainly in the hall, when a tall, darkly clad manservant appeared. He gazed momentarily at this fragile waif and sighed.

"Sir Nathan is expecting you," he said kindly, opening yet another large oak door for her.

The room seemed oppressive and gloomy, with a fire glowing despite the summer heat outside. At her entry, a man in a wheelchair turned to greet her. He was spare and white haired with an autocratic air. Morien felt an impulse to curtsey, she was so nervous, but his smile was welcoming as he indicated a chair beside him.

"Hello, Morien. I'm Renaldo's friend, Nathan," he said. Sitting down gingerly she returned his greeting.

"All a bit of a surprise?" he questioned. "I told Renaldo not to describe the place in too much detail in case it frightened you away."

"I think you were right, "responded Morien "I was expecting a cosy stable yard with a few old nags." Nathan roared with laughter.

"Would you like a drink before dinner? " He asked. Dinner! Heavens, how did one eat with a Sir? Suddenly she had no appetite. Images of her father flashed into her mind. Always lay the table for meals. Never succumb to eating from a tray on your lap. He was so meticulous – cutlery just so. Glasses for water, napkins. No need to be afraid now.

"No, no thank you." Morien stammered. "I don't really drink alcohol that often."

"In that case, we'll start straight away. Rankin, I think it would be less intimidating to serve dinner in here. Oh, and bring me light white wine." Rankin retreated with a smile.

"So, you are Morien. You've certainly grown since I last saw you. My old friend, Renaldo, told me of your plight." He smiled at her. "Losing your close ones is difficult." Morien looked away into the fire as memories flooded over her. " I was acquainted with Pavo, your father, although not very well –

20

different acts I suppose. The circus was on one of its European tours that we used to do in the winter in those days. I recall how he arrived, a refugee from some war. He was not like the rest of us, always a bit aloof. You were so small and cute but for almost a year no one could get you to speak. Of course, then you couldn't speak English. It was Renaldo with all his funny acts that eventually managed a breakthrough. But you were always withdrawn. I hope in some small way we can help you over your grief and prepare you to cope alone."

"You are very kind," murmured Morien as Rankin moved small tables around and covered them with food.

"Possibly a little selfish too. I sometimes yearn for the circus life, the smell of sawdust, the bustle of the one-night stands. When Renaldo telephoned, I simply couldn't resist having you here." Morien smiled nervously.

"Tell me about your act - about your father and the horses. I suppose it hasn't changed much since my time. What's Renaldo up to?"

Here was safe ground. Morien sparkled with animation as she described her old life, her expressive face and elegant hands conjuring up the scenes for the Earl's amusement. Then she told of her father's death how she had been propositioned and almost compromised and how Renaldo had helped her. How vividly she recalled that precious moment when Renaldo had given her the news of a new future.

"You should have seen Gino's face when I told him I was leaving." Morien smiled at Nathan "He really thought he'd got me." She ended her story with a note of triumph. "I can never thank Renaldo enough."

"Gino's always had a soft spot for a pretty woman," laughed the Earl. "There were times when I almost had to hide my wife. Renaldo told you about her did he and how I came to be stuck in this wretched chair?"

"Yes," said Morien "He told me very little, just the bare bones, how you lost your wife, and you're a good friend who owes him one." Not wanting to pry, she went on quickly. "Will you never walk again?" she asked boldly.

"That's what all the quacks say," he smiled

"With all these horses around have you never thought of riding? I'm told it's very therapeutic for people in wheelchairs," she asked shyly.

"I must confess I haven't," mused Nathan "Must have a word with Rankin. I know he goes out for a hack around the estate from time to time, so he can escort me. That would give them all a surprise down at the yard."

"Well, I think you should give it a try, there are all those lovely ponies in the yards. Then perhaps we could ride together," she said winningly. Nathan smiled. She was so refreshing.

"So, what do you think of our place so far?"

"Do you know, this will be the first time I've ever slept in a house, let alone had a room of my own?" she said seriously "It will be a strange sensation."

Nathan laughed aloud "I had the same feeling when I got home after having been on the road for so many years, but the novelty soon passes. But what of the stables and the girls?"

Morien paused. "Helen seems most efficient," she said carefully, "The estate, well I am overwhelmed. I nearly got lost when I arrived. It's more like a small village. I think I am going to need a street plan."

Her comment on Helen was not lost on Nathan but he felt Morien would cope. He smiled.

"Well, we do have such things as maps to help when repairs and suchlike are necessary, otherwise nothing would get done because the workers would be permanently lost. There are about 600 acres." He saw the question in her eyes.

"How could an injured circus performer come to have such a place?"

"I did wonder," she responded.

"Well, I inherited the estate when my elder brother was drowned in a sailing accident. You see, I hated this place when I was young as it would never be mine. I was a real black sheep setting off to find the most extremely different occupation there was. Freedom, excitement" his eyes reflected his memories, "When my wife died, I retreated here. There was nowhere else to go. This place was still here, in disrepair. My mother, God rest her, had done her best but there was no one competent to run the estate when she could no longer manage. My son still wasn't old enough." Morien was fascinated.

"It must have been an enormous load after the freedoms you'd had."

He became philosophical. "A new challenge, I suppose and, of course, I had my son, Drago. He had been living here with my mother. The circus is not really the best place to bring up a child."

Morien was indignant. "I disagree," she said. "I had the most wonderful childhood. And, I think children need their parents," she stated daringly.

"True but accidents happen, don't they?" Chastened, she acknowledged his comment. "My mother never really forgave me for my wildlife. She truly loved my brother, Quintin, although he was not a strong person, but he liked to be at home with her. After she lost him, I think having Drago living here helped her to have a reason to go on. She felt my injuries and loss of wife were my just deserts." Morien was shocked. Families to her were special and supportive. Seeing his preoccupation, she felt perhaps it was time for her to leave, when he suddenly looked up and said:

"Tell me about your horse."

"Merlin?"

"Yes. I like his name."

"He's a 5-year-old stallion my father bred from one of our mares. His paces and temperament were so well suited to our work that father kept him and trained him young. He simply adored 'dancing' to music in the circus."

"I suppose he has to work at quite a young age to earn his keep in your world."

"Oh yes. No idling. Well, you have given me such an opportunity. I can't think how to thank you."

"You can thank me by working hard and saying nothing of Renaldo or the circus to any of the people here." Morien looked startled and wondered what she had already said. "My son disapproves of the circus even though he knows little about it. Influenced by his grandmother. It took him a while to get used to having me at home. He tolerates me because I gave him the horses and helped him to get started here." He looked a little amused.

He took her hand "Promise me this."

"All right," vowed Morien gazing at him with great sincerity.

23

"A very pretty picture." Morien snatched her hand away and jumping up, stared transfixed at the tall, arrogant man in the doorway, divesting himself of his jacket. He dropped it on a chair and crossed the room like a panther, his lithe muscular grace carrying him soundlessly across the carpet.

"Why, Drago," exclaimed Nathan "This is a nice surprise. We didn't expect you back for a few more days."

"Evidently," said Drago meaningfully and Morien blushed to the roots of her hair at his obvious implications as he eyed her up and down.

"Morien, this is my son, Drago, often known as the Baron." He flashed a grin at Drago. Morien politely offered her hand. With a wicked grin, the Baron clicked his heels and holding her hand as Nathan did earlier, kissed it, playing with her fingers. He gazed under veiled eyelids up her arm and into her eyes. "Enchanted," he said. Morien recoiled, extracting her hand as his touch sent strange quiverings right through her body. He was like a powerful predator, the sort that fascinate and enthral before going for the kill. Everything about him exuded power. She noticed how his dark hair curled around his ears and the intensity of his deep brown eyes. She knew she was staring but could not tear her eyes away.

"Morien has come to us on the recommendation of an old friend." The Baron raised his eyebrows but said nothing. "I have arranged for her to start work in the yard."

At that Drago bristled. "Your mistress work? Why the subterfuge? You've never bothered about it in the past." He turned to Morien, "I hope you know of his reputation."

"You misunderstand me. Morien is here to work," said Nathan softly. The atmosphere was becoming highly charged. The Baron answered the challenge in his father's eyes.

"That is impossible. You know we have a waiting list. I have promised the first available vacancy to the Blackthorne-Smith girl." He looked angry. "You know it's political to ensure we get planning permission for the new indoor schools."

"That's not what Nina thinks, " returned Nathan

"I'll use whatever means I need." Drago scowled.

"She's coming for the short intensive course. Morien will be a working pupil."

"It cannot be. We don't need any more W.P.s. This is not a charity." Morien wished the ground would open as the argument got fiercer around her. She gazed fearfully at the Baron's aggressive aquiline face.

"Permit me to make my own decisions in my own establishment," said Nathan

"The house and farms, yes, the stables, no. They are my province."

"Come, Drago, we're embarrassing our guest," Nathan tried to placate him.

"Ah yes, your feminine company. Is this a new procedure - wining and dining prospective minions?" The Baron glanced scornfully at Morien.

"Drago " warned Nathan. "I am sorry, my dear, our pleasant evening together has been spoiled. My son is obviously tired."

Morien took her dismissal gratefully and fled from the room. Raised voices followed her across the hall. She couldn't bear it. All her newfound security seemed to have evaporated. She ran for comfort to Merlin's stable and clung to him.

"Oh, Merlin," she wept. "Nobody wants us. Please, God, don't let them send us away."

CHAPTER 4

Despite the traumas of the previous evening, Morien woke early as usual. It took her a moment to orientate herself. She was no longer in the caravan. Realisation hit her and the angry face of the Baron flashed into her mind. Had she jumped from the frying pan into the fire? Her stomach churned. She forced herself out of bed and quickly showered. A bathroom to herself was another new luxury. She surveyed herself in the mirror, flicking back her honey hair. Though it did not register with her, even in an old pair of jeans she had style. Her slim figure was almost boyish under the open necked shirt. Tucking it in she fastened her belt emphasising her slim waistline.

Taking a deep breath, she headed out the door and ran down the stairs fortunately remembering Helen's directions. The place was quite a maze. At the door, she hesitated then. Could she do this? Her heart was beating overtime; her hands were clammy. No choice said her inner voice. Taking a deep breath, she stepped over the threshold holding her head high. As she entered the dining room the occupants stared bleary eyed. It was a bright room with a kitchen down one side. Food, cereals, fruit, milk, toast were ranged across a large side table. There were several girls sitting at the pine tables with chintzy tablecloths. Morien paused and carefully assessed the procedure. Seems we help ourselves she thought and joined the small queue. Certainly, a change from the solitude of the last few weeks. She grabbed an apple and spooned some yogurt into a bowl.

Gill was already there. She called Morien over and made the introductions. Morien balancing her tray made her way over.

"This is Morien – Rosemary, Elizabeth, Jeremy, Freddie, Sue," said Gill. Each nodded a welcome. "All W.P.s - working pupils," she said "the first shift. The snotty lot all get an extra half hour in bed." She humphed into a corner table.

"Who are the snotty lot, Gill?" asked Morien joining her.

"Oh, they are the paying students. They usually come for about six months to get their teaching qualifications. It's a more concentrated course and quite expensive. Not like us W.P.s who have to work for a living while we get qualified."

Morien went back to the counter for a cup of tea when she was waylaid.

"You intending to go out on the yard dressed like that?" queried Sue, a plumpish fair girl, munching her way through a mountain of toast.

"Er, yes," said Morien looking down at her somewhat tired jeans. She'd put on her wellie boots anticipating a stint mucking out the stables.

"Well, you can't," said Sue emphatically. "Helen will have a fit. Don't you have any proper gear?"

"I'er .." she nearly blurted out - my circus clothes. "I usually wear chaps over my jeans when I ride," said Morien

"Chaps!" exclaimed Christine, a tall weedy female "This is Wilton Hall, not the Old T Ranch." Everyone laughed as Morien blushed.

"You obviously didn't read all the literature before you signed the dotted line. Clothing was almost the priority – worse than school," commented Sue.

"This is all I've got," said Morien firmly "so it'll have to do, till my trunk arrives," she fabricated. There were some scornful noises. Gill came to her rescue.

"I've put on so much weight since I've been here. All this awful food! You're in luck, I've just had to buy a new pair of jodhs. Cost all last month's money. I'll sell you my old ones."

"That's kind," exclaimed Morien in relief feeling as though she had been sitting on a coconut shy.

"Don't forget you'll need a hat when you ride," said Jeremy helpfully.

Morien nearly asked what kind of hat then covered herself by exclaiming "Bother, I knew there was something I'd left behind."

"Never mind. There's a collection in the tack room we use for clients who've forgotten theirs."

Morien munched her way through her apple trying to work out how long, at this rate, her meagre finances were going to last. She surreptitiously examined the outfits around her - jodhpurs, long boots, waistcoats. She realised that she had absolutely no idea of the cost of such clothing. It was laughable but she didn't even know where to go to buy it. How could she ask without raising suspicions? From Gill's comment about new stuff, it sounded expensive. She regretted her promise to the Earl.

Everyone would have understood if they knew her background. What a tangle. Well at least she was going to get some pocket money and, at the end of all this she should be employable. She tried not to feel bleak as she went to attend to Merlin.

The morning had brightened, and the air was fresh from overnight rain. All around her was a feeling of slow awakening as the machine of the yard gradually came to life. Merlin whickered as she approached, and she noticed his eyes were bright with interest in his new surroundings. He was also having the treat of a permanent roof and a deep comfortable bed. No more canvas stables on damp grass. She refreshed his hay and water and then dashed to the main yard. It was 6.30 a.m.

The other girls were already working with their allotted horses and Helen was pinning up the "Orders for the Day". She explained its purpose to Morien. "It is a general aide memoire," she said. "On it you will find details of all the events for the day. The horses needed for lessons are listed against the times they are required with the names of the clients and the grooms responsible. If you're riding yourself, you bring your allocated mount to the indoor school at the time listed here, and don't be late."

Morien surveyed the list in awe.

"It all looks rather complicated," she murmured. Helen ignored the comment

"There is a secondary list showing feeding times, tack cleaning, stable management lectures etc. You are expected at lectures when not needed elsewhere. All these items are fitted into a strict timetable, and you must adhere to it. With the number of horses, clients and students it is the only way to keep things running smoothly." This was obviously a big business thought Morien. Not a two-bit hack hire run on love and cash.

As the morning progressed, Morien began to see that this was like co-ordinating a circus with all the different acts and many performers. They were always having crises because Gino couldn't delegate, nor could he do everything himself. He would have done better using such a system, she thought. A lot of the muddles would have been avoided. Maybe even the lion would not have escaped.

"Are you listening?" Helen's voice cut in. "I'm told that you have many years' experience in horse care so I've allocated you

Puffin and Whisper. Come and meet them. You will be entirely responsible for their welfare under my supervision." They walked through to the outer stable blocks, near the field pony lines. About ten to twelve ponies, very muddy, in all shapes and sizes, looking very shaggy in the remains of their winter coats were being brought in from the fields.

"As I mentioned before these ponies are very quiet to ride and are used mainly for young children and beginners and, of course, the disabled riders." Helen explained. "They take a lot of cleaning each day though. They seem to revel in the mud, but they are strong and extremely compassionate and remarkably understanding of the riders in their care." As they walked on to the main stable block, Morien thought of her comment to Nathan and wondered if he'd take it up.

"Here we are. This is Puffin." Puffin was a grey cob whose mane had been trimmed very short. "He's been hogged as he suffers from sweet itch. You'll need to treat it from time to time." said Helen. He seemed to have a wicked eye. Whisper, on the other hand, was a slender bay about sixteen hands tall. She seemed gentle and friendly. Morien was right in her assessment of Puffin who attempted to bite as they passed his box.

"The daily routine never varies," said Helen "First, water and then check your horse for overnight injuries or signs of illness. Next, feed and muck out followed by grooming and exercise when the food has been digested. "You will notice that many of the horses are stabled on deep litter. Are you familiar with that?"

"Not really. We always bedded down on new straw." Morien just stopped herself from explaining why deep litter was unsuitable for animals constantly on the move.

"Here we provide a deep but soft bed which is skipped out regularly during the day to remove dropping and wet areas. It's economical and the horses seem to like it. The skips are those shallow square things over there." She indicated a stack of black rubberish items. "Remember to check when your horses are required in the school and .." Helen went on and on. Morien began to feel saturated. It wasn't that she didn't know what to do, it was all the military type rules.

Helen left her. After that everything seemed to go wrong. Morien felt panicky. She couldn't find a wheelbarrow or any mucking out tools. Had she missed this information from Helen?

Desperately looking for possible hidey holes she eventually found an ally in Gill who introduced her to all the mysteries that were so confusing.

"They're kept over here in this lean-to. I thought it was crackers when I first came," confided Gill "but without such clear directions and everything in its proper place it would be a shambles, especially with people like me." She laughed, then suddenly began to sweep the yard with an excess of vigour as the Baron appeared leading a magnificent chestnut horse back to its stable.

He looked even more elegant and masculine in his riding clothes, topped with a rakish soft trilby. Beautifully cut breeches hugged slim hips and his boots glistened on his elegant legs. Morien felt her heart trip. She was fascinated by him - the power, the grace, oh and the fear.

"Gossiping again, Gill" he said curtly.

"Just explaining things to the newcomer," smiled Gill with a toss of her short curls.

"The newcomer? Ah yes." His eyes flicked over Morien who muttered 'good morning' and retreated into Whisper's stable. The Baron disappeared into the main yard only to emerge some minutes later with a dancing bay horse, heading once more for the indoor school. She observed him over the stable door. Never had she come across such eye-catching charisma. Well, at least, nothing had been said so far about sending her away. She let out a deep sigh of relief as she watched his retreat - the lithe confident strides as he led the prancing horse away.

"It's safe to come out now," laughed Gill as the sound of hooves receded. "The Baron rides all the advanced horses that come in for schooling," she explained. "He normally starts about six with his own horse, Iatro, that's the chestnut one. The school is used for lessons for most of the day, so he has to cram a lot in before ten. Helen and some of the senior students exercise early in the outdoor arenas. Later they school the less experienced horses under his eagle eye."

Morien was relieved to have some idea of his timetable so she could be sure to avoid him. Somehow, she got through the morning without making too many mistakes, dodging Puffin's persistent ugly teeth, nasty bit of work!

CHAPTER 5

Then Gill surprised her bringing a message from Helen that she was to have an assessment lesson immediately after lunch on Puffin. "I'll drop the jodhpurs in your room when I go for lunch," promised Gill.

Morien rushed down to Merlin's stable. So far, she hadn't had time to attend to him properly. If she had to present herself in the school at 2.00p.m. she had a bare hour. She mucked out rather cursorily and led Merlin out to stretch his legs and nibble at the grass verge. Several mares with foals came prancing over to the fence to see him. He glanced up and whickered but then disinterestedly continued to graze. Despite still being a stallion, he had been handled properly since birth and rarely misbehaved. Anyway, the mares apparently weren't in season so there was nothing to rouse him. Morien petted one of the mares whose foal nuzzled for milk. What paradise this place was - the space, the freedom of it all. The safe wooden fencing – no nasty barbed wire, horses able to run free in the paddocks. The circus horses had been permanently haltered on the rare occasions that they found free grass. As she drank in all the beauty around her, the clock chimed. Panic - the time! She persuaded the reluctant Merlin to leave the grass. He pranced a little and called to the mares, one of which floated along the fence beside him, tail held high. The beauty of her movement enraptured Morien.

"Back in the box with you." She ushered Merlin protesting into the stable, checked the hay and water and then dashed for the house to change.

Gill's jodhpurs were a bit on the large size for Morien's slim figure. She was going to need a belt or something. There was no way they were going to stay up alone. She rummaged through her possessions for something suitable. She found some brightly patterned braces, substituted for a lack of a belt. With her wellies that she always used for mucking out at the circus, she didn't look too odd. The earlier jibe about the Old T Ranch flashed through her head but what the heck. With a final brush through her honey locks, she didn't realise what a gamin picture she made as she hurried out to the yard. Finding Puffin's gear, she tacked him up, trying to avoid being bitten at every turn.

She arrived at the indoor school just in time for her lesson.

"Where's your hat?" asked Helen, then impatiently "Here give me Puffin and get one from the tack room. And run."

Morien fled. In the tack room, she rummaged in the pile of hats. Too big, too small. Oh, bother who cares? She crammed one on her head and rushed back to the school where Helen immediately pulled the brim down to her nose like an army officer. "I suppose you'll do," she murmured handing over Puffin. The school was a very large enclosed and roofed area with a soft surface. Around the walls it was lined at the lower level with planking above which, placed at intervals, were enormous mirrors.

Morien was just taking all this in when, to her surprise, the Baron appeared, a picture of sophistication, looking even more magnificent in his soft brown trilby and a long coat over his riding clothes. Morien was startled. The whole of her insides churned. So now it was going to come - her dismissal. Fear clutched at her as he looked her up and down. Her clothing now seemed totally ridiculous, compared with the other girls and his elaborately formal attire.

His supercilious gaze held her like a mesmerised rabbit. Never in her life had another person affected her so. It's just because he holds my future, she thought to reassure herself. She forced herself to walk naturally towards him, but the horse caught her jitters and jibbed irritatingly.

Morien felt his thoughts, his irritation. She was unnerved as his glance swept over her.

"Good afternoon," he said doffing his hat with an elegant gesture. She wondered fleetingly if she was expected to bow too as she nervously responded to his greeting with a slight dip.

"Would you kindly mount."

Hurriedly, Morien got into the saddle and checked the girth and stirrups, whilst the Baron waited, lightly tapping his boot with a long riding whip. He studied her lissom body, neat, tiny breasts and buttocks. Where had his father found her? He had to admit that he had quite good taste when it came to pretty girls.

"The purpose of this session is for the rider to demonstrate her ability and for me to make an assessment of what that rider needs to be taught." he looked scathingly into her eyes as he enunciated the last few words with a particular emphasis. Morien flushed as she got his meaning and was rewarded with a sardonic twitch from the corner of his mouth.

"Have you ridden inside before?" he enquired.

"Not in a school," admitted Morien, thinking of the circus ring. She was hypnotised by his penetrating eyes.

"Then I will explain the rules of the road as it were."

Morien tried to keep her attention on his words. Relief that the axe had not fallen was mingled with an overwhelming feeling of weakness in the face of this dominant personality. How could the gentle and considerate Earl have produced such an impersonal monster?

She examined his aristocratic features and the way he carried his head - oh so proud. The long coat, although flowing and ostentatious, could not be bettered. The way he flicked his whip against his free hand sent chills through her. What was he talking about? Since he'd gone on for some length, Morien's brain refused to take in anymore.

"Are you listening?" he interrupted her thoughts. "So, to the track walk march and take the right rein," he commanded. Morien urged Puffin forward. Nothing happened. She tried again. Again, no response. She heard a soft sigh and met a bored glance, so she gave Puffin a boot in the ribs which he couldn't doubt, and he jumped forward. What a funny horse, what was the matter with him? she wondered.

She was asked to show the horse's paces on both reins, stop, start, turn around until she hardly knew whether she was coming or going. Like a sergeant major the Baron imperiously ordered her this way and that. Puffin was obedient but lethargic and heavy which Morien couldn't understand. Her father's horses had never felt like that but responded to the lightest touch. On this horse, when she wanted to stop instead of a light body tension, she had to pull on the reins. To change pace, she had to kick hard and making him bend around corners was impossible, like riding on a board.

Morien felt so insecure, terrified that she would go the wrong way or misunderstand as he rapped orders at her. "I must not make any mistake," she thought. "or give him any excuse to get rid of me."

Then suddenly she realised she was not really in charge of Puffin because of her nervousness and her thoughts being split between the horse and the Baron. She became quite cross with herself and brought the horse to the halt. Puffin knew immediately that he had been rumbled and came to attention. Morien then really made him dance to her tune and he was 100% responsive. She knew the Baron's attitude had also changed and he had become attentive. "I'll damn well show you. At least I can prove I know about horses, even if they are great lumps." she thought uncharitably. Puffin almost began to sparkle as she made him work correctly.

The Baron called her to the halt and approached with Helen who had returned whilst Morien was riding around. Morien found she was holding her breath as he advanced so aware was she of his magnetism. He did not look at her so again she had a chance to study him. It wasn't fair. He had far more than his share of good looks. Pity he didn't have some charm to go with them.

"You'll notice," he commented to Helen, " that she has a good natural seat with exceptional balance." Morien felt like a fly on the wall as they discussed her. "I'm here," her mind screamed.

"However, the lower leg is too far forward." He held her leg to manipulate it to a better position. Fire rushed through her as he swung her leg backwards, then eased it forward pushing her lower leg in close contact with the horse. Morien immediately wanted to withdraw it from his grip.

"Now, come on, relax," he commanded.

"At least she doesn't grip up when cantering," said Helen

"No, that's useful, but the rein contact is atrocious," he responded. "Do you understand contact?" Touching her leg, his eyes bored into hers at the double entendre as he went on to explain. To Morien, who frequently rode without any reins at all, it all seemed desperately complicated. She looked perplexed until he said exasperatedly, "It's like a tube of toothpaste with the lid on. You wind it up from the bottom until the contents are squeezed against the cap. This creates the power. The bit in the horse's mouth, like the lid, is always there without pulling backwards." Whilst he demonstrated with one hand on the rein, the other absently stroked Puffin's neck. Morien watched those strong, elegant fingers and momentarily felt envious of Puffin. Briefly she wondered what they felt like. She looked away. What was the matter with her?

He turned again to Helen. Together they moved her legs about as though she were a puppet, tilting her pelvis back and forth, shortening and lengthening the reins, explaining this and that until she felt completely wooden. It all seemed very mysterious. Every time the Baron touched her a shooting flame went through her. She was sure that he must be aware of it as she caught him giving her a quizzical look and burned with embarrassment. She simply wasn't used to being touched in this semi-intimate manner which all seemed so casually commonplace to him. A sudden memory of Gino shot through her.

Then the Baron asked her once more to show her paces in the new position. It was incredible at first. Her boots kept hooking under the saddle flaps and the saddle itself forced her to slump back again.

"Hold the front of the saddle," he ordered, "but keep your arm relaxed."

She felt like a useless child. "What have I let myself in for?" she worried.

At last, they let her go with a parting shot from the Baron "And kindly make sure you are properly turned out in future." He once again swept his hat from his head in dismissal. As she turned to go, she heard him say: "She obviously has reasonable experience for she got quite a tune out of Puffin, you know how indescribably lazy he is." She intrigued Drago. Here was a natural talent.

She escaped humiliated. Why was he so horrid? Was this how he treated all the new pupils? Perhaps it was and she was being too sensitive. She had always been praised for her riding by all who knew her and to be moulded into some sort of straitjacket to please the Baron went greatly against the grain. She felt her chagrin rising and unkindly took it out on Puffin. "You're more like a camel than a horse," she complained "all piggy and hard work." Irritatingly her livelihood depended on obeying instructions, and she couldn't offend the Earl. She would just have to stomach it all.

As she returned Puffin to his box, she noticed the disabled ride just leaving the pony lines. She saw Helen going over to inspect looking a little worried. There at the back with a solicitous Rankin was Nathan looking exceedingly pleased with himself. Their eyes met and he winked at her. Just in time she

35

remembered not to respond, but Helen noticed and gave her a quizzical look. Morien felt laughter bubbling up inside her as she untacked Puffin. "I wonder how the Baron feels about his father taking up riding or even if he knows."

She mused until her work for the day was done and she took a bridle down to Merlin's box. She led him out and vaulted up lightly bareback, setting off towards the paddocks. She didn't dare go near the school, not that she wanted to anyway. After Puffin, Merlin was poetry in motion. Merlin seemed to think he was on holiday and danced and spooked in a playful manner, so she asked for a brisk walk up the track to a large expanse of parkland and gave him a stretch. The big horse gradually lengthened his stride, letting out all his pent-up energy in an exhilarating gallop. Morien lay along his neck relishing the speed and the freedom. Returning refreshed she was daydreaming happily when a voice said curtly "Get off that horse." She turned in horror to the Baron.

"I said, get off that horse." She couldn't believe her ears. What on earth was the matter now. She looked at him defiantly, a diminutive elf on the great stallion. What a trouble this child was. Drago sighed and re-iterated with gentle menace "Get off that horse." She slid to the ground, and he towered over her. "Never again will you ride on my land without a hat."

"Even on my own horse," she retorted angrily.

"Even on your own horse, well-mannered though he appears to be." He cast an expert eye over Merlin, who nuzzled him gently. Morien pulled the horse away sharply, afraid that he would soil the immaculate sleeve, but the Baron gently stroked the stately head. They were standing so close that Morien could feel his aura of strength and maleness. He transferred his hand to her hair and flicked it lightly. "You should not risk that pretty head," he said. "Anyway, my insurance would not cover you which would upset my father wouldn't it?"

"Just what are you insinuating," cried Morien her ire truly up.

"Come, come, coquin. I have the evidence of my own eyes." His scorn showed. "Grandmama warned of my father's propensity for unsuitable women. Always a roving eye. Till now, he's had his affairs elsewhere. This is too close to home and . he's worth a pretty penny, isn't he?" He turned abruptly away and strode towards the house.

36

Morien again felt as though she had been touched by fire and her face burned from his personal insult. How dare he, and bossing her around like this on her own horse. She'd conform on his, but never on hers. To hell with his insurance. And that quip about his father and money - it was just about the nastiest thing she'd ever heard. Disgruntled she bedded down the horse and took her anger out on the straw until Merlin snorted with perplexity.

"Sorry, old boy," she muttered "He makes me so mad. He's so rude. I guess I'm just hungry." She tried to rationalise to herself, but she could not put into words the effect that he had on her physically. How she longed to tell him how wrong he was, that she was just an orphaned circus girl. But, her promise to Nathan stood.

She tried to get Drago out of her mind, but his image wouldn't go. She wondered whether to confide in Nathan that Drago's suspicions that they were having an affair were continuing. She felt that Nathan had dismissed it as the myth it was without further thought. Why was he so insulting to his father? Was he so indoctrinated by his grandmother that he was incapable of forming his own opinions? There obviously was a deep bitterness. She couldn't conceive what his childhood could have been like without a father, for hers had been so secure, despite being itinerant. Drago's grandmother had certainly poisoned his mind and, what of his mother who had died? Was there something about her that had made the marriage unsuitable? She decided there were too many questions. She would have to find out if the opportunity arose since it could explain his attitude towards her. She tried to imagine him as a young boy. Did he feel deserted, was this what had hardened his heart? She tried to visualise the Earl's mother, also deserted. Her first son dead and her second injured. All her hopes pinned on her arrogant grandson.

Eventually, locking the stable door she made her way to the main house and, having devoured an enormous meal of stodge, crawled thankfully into bed setting her alarm for 5.00 a.m. so that she could exercise Merlin before work. Her sleep was disturbed by dreams of appearing for lessons dressed in her circus spangles and being sent away in disgrace.

37

She awoke feeling sluggish. The beautiful morning alive with the dawn chorus soon cast its spell. As she dressed, she remembered that clothing was going to be a problem. Now, however, it just had to be jeans and trainers so she could go and see to Merlin.

He nickered as she approached, the early morning air making small clouds of his breath. Morien gave him a few carrots and a quick brush over before leading him out in just a bridle. She vaulted on bareback and set off at a brisk pace down the dew-laden path. Everywhere was magic. Overnight the spiders had been doing overtime and cascades of jewels covered every bush. They sparkled invitingly. The air was clear and cool so she could see the church spire in the far distance, outlined against the distant Downs. In all directions were beautifully kept fields with wooden fencing, some with mares and foals, some with cattle.

She suddenly realised that this was another first for her. In the circus, such early morning outings were the prerogative of her father. She usually worked first and rode later. He was a stickler for routine always saying that you couldn't tell a horse that his breakfast was late because you'd overslept.

"They are animals of habit and have an internal clock that is minutely accurate."

Her mind turned to the Baron. Was he just getting up? An image of him all tousled from sleep presented itself although it was difficult to visualise him as anything less than immaculate. Did he wear pyjamas? Yes, probably silk ones, she thought enviously as she remembered her old cotton T-shirt, certainly a different class from her. Her reverie was broken by the chiming from the clock tower over the stable yard and retracing her steps through the soothing countryside she returned quickly, refreshed Merlin's water and hay and dashed for breakfast.

After several days, she began to get used to things. The early morning rides stimulated her. Her confidence began to return as she realised that nothing was really new, it was just done slightly differently or given a different name. Also, she began to understand the hierarchy with the working pupils, like herself, right at the very bottom. The paying students lorded it over them often leaving the W.P.s to do the heavy work and clear up the mess in the yard and feed rooms.

At least she was getting lessons most days, not with the Baron but with Helen who was much more understanding and Morien liked her. Some days she was allowed to ride Whisper which was great as the mare was much more responsive and really seemed to listen to Morien's aids. The trouble was that Whisper was so popular with the clients that often her only choice was the indomitable Puffin. The worst part for Morien were the stable management lectures. They were boring and impossible. All that bookwork and what for? She wasn't cut out for it. Going out and doing it was what mattered to the horses. Would she survive she wondered?

After a particularly galling day when another of the new paying intake had insulted her attire mercilessly, Morien flopped out on her bed and cried her eyes out. She had been making excuses that there was no time to go shopping that her trunk hadn't arrived, so she had to earn the money first. They had nicknamed her Huckleberry Finn and frequently sniggered as she passed.

"Who's the hillbilly? Riding in wellies – I don't believe it." They were too nasty. "Why did they behave so badly," she thought. "Didn't their fathers teach them anything?" She simply was not used to cattiness. What a protected life she had led. It happened in the circus but in a friendlier way as in families - not this unembellished cutting edge.

Gill had tried to support her, but the old class barriers even pushed her onto the side-lines, especially since Morien was so secretive about her origins. She realised that her promise to Nathan was actually isolating her.

Tearfully she dragged herself to the dressing table to try to repair her ravaged appearance when she discovered a note tucked underneath her hairbrush.

"Come and see me this evening at 9.00 p.m." It was signed by the Earl.

Panic stricken she realised it was already 9.00 p.m. Hurriedly she threw on a pair of cleaner jeans and scraped back her hair into a ponytail. As she ran for the main house the image of the Baron crossed her mind. A flash fired her which she mistook for fear of seeing him. Rankin was hovering as she appeared.

"Ah, come this way, miss." She smiled at his solicitous manner as she realised that he had probably been responsible for the delivery of the note. Nathan was waiting impatiently for her.

"See that we are not disturbed, Rankin," he commanded to the butler's retreating back. Rankin smiled. "We don't want a repeat of our last experience," grinned Nathan conspiratorially.

"Tell me how you are settling in." He gazed indulgently at the sylph sitting before him. Even unadorned she had charm, a transient elusiveness. Her eyes had a sparkle and looked greener than ever. She had obviously been crying.

Morien responded to his fatherly warmth and shared her hopes, doubts and fears. "It was all so confusing to start with." she acknowledged. "I felt such a fool, as though I had suddenly arrived in a foreign land. Now I know it's just what I have been doing all my life, with a few embellishments."

"I'm glad you're finding your feet. And your horse, is he all right?"

"Yes, although his schooling is in abeyance for the time being. I suppose a rest won't hurt him."

"It's often beneficial in the early stages," said Nathan "You should keep lunging him though to keep the flexibility." Morien looked thoughtful. "How are your lessons going?" He wanted her version. He had already had chapter and verse from the frustrated Baron. He was extremely amused at the constant mention of her. He couldn't decide whether it was just anger, a deliberate attempt to pique or a hidden interest. He smiled as he recalled Drago's exasperation and masked demands to know more about Morien.

"Her talent is exceptional," he'd acknowledged grudgingly, "but it is not classical."

"There are many ways of achieving," responded the Earl. "Maybe you should look more carefully."

"It's a long time since I've seen Puffin go so well," Drago had said. "At first, I thought she was just a star struck wimp when Puffin hardly moved. Then, suddenly she took charge, and he went like an angel. I could do a lot with such talent."

Nathan had smiled. "Feel free." The reaction should have been expected. He'd put his foot in it.

"I'd forgotten," sneered Drago "There are, of course, others much more worthy of my time," he'd said

40

Nathan brought his thoughts back to the present.

"Oh, I'm such a mutton head," she laughed "Me, who can stand on a horse's rump whilst it canters around the ring, vault on and off, and ride all the fancy advanced stuff bareback, am completely useless on a saddle. I don't know how your son puts up with me. He never stops nagging."

Nathan smiled. This was a good sign, it confirmed she did have some talent for Drago to bother. Put together with Drago's endless absorption with the subject of her confirmed his suspicion that his son was not just putting the needle in him. Drago had taken the bait, as he hoped he would, accepting the circus world wasn't all bad. It really was going to be fascinating when the secret came out, but that would have to wait until Drago had ridden her horse.

"Drago is fascinated with the classical training of horses. The end product can be quite like the circus, but the training methods are radically different."

Morien was perplexed.

"He was one of the lucky ones selected to go to the Spanish Riding School in Vienna. He went from there to the French School in Saumur. He considers circus training to be all tricks and punishments."

"That is rubbish." Morien flashed angrily.

"You and I know that," said Nathan. "You just use different methods but, in the end, you still work with your weight. The outcome is the same, but I cannot shift his view. He is sometimes very bigoted. The nagging is just constant little reminders to keep everything together."

"Yes, I suppose so."

"Drago works rather like a sculptor, visually shaping the horse's movement. He anticipates problems, sees them beginning to form and corrects them before they can fully develop. This is rare talent – to have such an eye for movement."

"You're proud of him," said Morien

"Oh yes, but it would never do to let him know," was the rejoinder.

No. thought Morien two proud people!

"I saw you had ventured out riding. How did you get on?"

41

"Can't imagine why I've never done it before," responded the Earl. "Fortunately, Rankin was brought up with horses so he can take care of me. I really enjoyed the independence of it."

"Will your son object?"

"Don't care if he does, after all I did help him buy his first few horses."

"Tell me about his mother," she ventured.

"Alison." His eyes misted "Perhaps she was my biggest mistake, so full of life and sparkle. A little sylph like you."

"And your family didn't approve of her?"

"Oh, she was well enough bred, aristocratic. Everyone was delighted with our marriage, the future settled. But she was a wild cap like me. We got this crazy idea to run away and join the circus. I encouraged her to defect and look what happened."

"But you had a good life together," said Morien

"Yes, but my mother never forgave us for returning to the circus after Drago was born. She insisted he stayed with her, his grandmother, since the family and the estate came first. Alison was such an "unsuitable" mother, especially when she named the child Drago after some distant Slavic ancestor."

"Didn't you want to take Drago with you then?"

"Not really. He was better off at home, and I think Alison truly loved her free life. It was the perfect solution." Morien looked sad.

"Enough of an old man's maunderings. Now, since everything seems to be going so well, perhaps you will tell me what you were crying about earlier. Your eyes gave you away when you first came in." Morien turned away and blinked hard as the wave of misery returned.

"Oh, it's nothing, she murmured

"I'm afraid I cannot accept that, said Nathan "They obviously weren't brief tears."

"I wear all the wrong clothes," burst out Morien. "We didn't have all this fancy gear, just jeans and chaps and spangles. Gill has sold me an outgrown pair of jodhs. but they only fit where they touch and everyone else is so immaculate and they keep teasing me and calling me names." A vision of the Baron sprang up before her. "Even when I get paid, I won't be able to do more than pay Gill and the Baron is insisting that I dress correctly for my lessons." Morien hung her head, despair written all over her. How she hated to admit her poverty.

"How remiss of me," said Nathan "I forgot Drago's obsession with turnout. Although to be fair, it is a fetish throughout the horse world. A hangover from army days I believe." He thought for a moment. He knew he could not offer her money. She was too proud and besides, she would feel obligated to return it. He had a sudden thought. Of course ..

"I think I have a solution. Call Rankin for me will you." Nathan looked pleased with himself as Morien went to the door. Rankin must have been on guard outside for he came immediately.

"Ah, Rankin. I think you know where to find my late wife's riding clothes. Will you bring them down?" Turning towards Morien "There seems little sense in their mouldering away in a cupboard. I never could be bothered to sort her things out." Morien could see the old pain in his eyes.

Within a few minutes, Rankin returned. "How about these boots," said Nathan "My wife was about your size."

Morien removed the trees from the boots of exquisite soft leather which looked almost unworn and tried them on. "Why, they are like gloves." She walked up and down getting used to them whilst Nathan looked on delightedly.

"Here try on this jacket." He handed her a smooth lightweight tweed. It proved to be the most perfect fit. She surveyed the effect in the mirror. It could have been made for her. As she fastened the buttons the expensively cut fabric moulded her lissom figure.

"They fit so well; I want you to have them." Eyes shining Morien flung her arms around him and hugged him.

"Steady on, now," he said gruffly

"You're wonderful," breathed Morien "What a gift."

"I'm glad you like them." He looked nostalgic as memories flooded back to him.

"Like them," exclaimed Morien ecstatically. She twirled up and down.

"Well, I'm glad they fit. Look there's a black jacket for formal occasions gloves, several pairs of breeches and a hat."

Suddenly becoming sober Morien said "I've never had such clothes before. Are you absolutely sure that you want to give them to me?"

"Of course. As you can see, they are hardly worn. They were bought for formal occasions when we came home. We had no need for them in the circus as you know so they hold no important memories."

"I am glad. I never want to hurt you." She twirled around again. "They are so beautiful. How am I going to explain them to the others?" Nathan looked pensive and then said, "How about - you just received a parcel from your aunt?" They both laughed.

Nathan glanced at the clock "Well, my dear, you'd better run along now since I am expecting Drago shortly and he's always punctual." Morien hugged him again. "Thank you, thank you, thank you."

CHAPTER 7

She was over the moon as she danced out of the room into the hall, clothes bundled against her, still wearing the jacket and boots straight into the arms of the Baron. They were both startled, and he pushed her out to arm's length. How long had he been standing there, she wondered?

"You again," he hissed "This is going too far." He steered her down the corridor and through the dividing door. "I'll not have you coming here and seducing my father. It's disgusting."

Morien remained silent, astounded at his accusations. He still held her and the response from her body was beyond her comprehension. What was coursing through her veins and why did he have this effect on her? She shrank back as he placed his hands on the wall encasing her, his face hovering just above hers. She could feel his breath on her cheeks and his nearness began to overwhelm her.

"What? Nothing to say, miss?" he taunted. She ducked and attempted to run, but he caught her again and once more pinned her to the wall. "What's it like kissing a man old enough to be your father?" he asked scornfully his face only inches from hers.

She was hypnotised, her eyes fastened on his slowly advancing lips. She felt a treacherous response and tried to wriggle away. "Playing the tease?" he taunted "You can't fool me." He leaned towards her again, repeating his insinuation, drawing her hips hard against his. "No" screamed her mind, "Yes" screamed her body.

Then, just as suddenly he dropped her, so she nearly fell. "Leave my father alone," he sneered.

Memories of Gino flooded her. Morien was outraged. Drawing herself up, she slapped him.

"You dirty minded prig," she stuttered as he angrily rubbed his cheek, her finger marks showing a red blaze across his shave line. "Keep your filthy thoughts and hands to yourself." Clasping the clothes to her chest she ran through to her room, knowing he could hardly follow her into the hostel area. She'd felt her reaction was justified, but would he? Would he let her stay after this encounter?

She leaned against her door feeling completely drained apart from her burning nerve ends. She'd been excited and repulsed. How had he the audacity to think such thoughts and spy on his father to boot? Well, he could keep well away from her, she vowed as she slipped out of the jacket. Somehow the gift seemed unaccountably spoiled. It was ironical, she thought, that she should be here to escape Gino and now find herself in a far more compromising situation.

Gino had been a massive danger but physically he had no effect on her. It was fear of his brutality that froze her in his company. Also, in the circus, they all looked after their own and she had protection on all sides. Of course, there was a parallel in that both men held her future in their hands and here she was helpless until she qualified. She couldn't keep running to Nathan like she had to Renaldo. She wished she could blot out the image of the Baron.

Her mind went back to those brief moments of body against body and her whole being tingled. "I must be rational" she thought. "I see him too frequently to melt like a ninny every time he appears." She'd heard other girls in the circus talking of being in love and had thought they were behaving like idiots. Now she was beginning to understand how ignorant her superiority was and regretted having paid so little attention to the girlish chatter.

It wasn't as though she didn't know about the sexual side, since she had been involved with her father's breeding programme – taking the mares to stud and helping with the pregnancies and births. What she knew nothing about was the emotional side, the total irrational behaviour and out of character responses. Chemistry, she had heard it called. Now it had attacked her. Even simple thoughts evoked responses, sneaking up on her unannounced. Her brush with Gino had not prepared her for this.

Alas, Drago had stimulated her so much she could not sleep. Every time she closed her eyes, he stood before her, eyes mocking, sending strange, flickering surges through to her soul – his style, his elegance, his total autocracy fascinated her. As the hours of sleeplessness dragged on, she decided to creep out and talk to Merlin. Despite it being the middle of the night, he whickered a welcome. In the warmth of the stable with the peaceful munch, munch, munch, Morien gradually felt at peace again. After all, despite the Baron's anger on the first night, he hadn't sent her away. Let's hope he doesn't now, she prayed.

The stars seemed extra bright as she made her way back. Rounding the main stable block, she heard a persistent banging coming from the main yard and decided to investigate since there didn't appear to be anyone else about. The noise seemed to be coming from the far side. She glanced into each box as she passed. Everything was well until she reached the middle box. There was the Baron's special chestnut, Iatro, completely cast against the back wall. He'd obviously gone down for a good roll and had got stuck, needing much more space to get enough impetus to swing over and get to his feet. He seemed to have been on his back struggling to get up for some time as he was sweating profusely. His thrashing had caused a small valley to form between the bedding and the wall that he'd fallen into. Morien found there was no way she could roll him over so that he could scramble to his feet. He was just too large. She'd have to get help. She went to the tack room to call Helen on the intercom. It rang and rang. There was no answer. A quick look at the duty list revealed it to be Helen's night off - "In absence of Senior Staff, tel. the Baron on extension 21". A frission of fear flowed through her at the irony of the situation as she rang the extension. This was no time for personal antagonism, a horse was in trouble.

His curt voice answered immediately. "Who's this?"

"Morien."

"Ah Looking for a little more medicine? You know it's the middle of the night? A bit cheeky after your last response."

Morien gasped. "Yours is the emergency number. I had no choice but to ring you." There was a pregnant silence. "I'm at the yard. Iatro's in trouble. He's cast in his box." She explained the crisis. "I've tried everything but cannot get him up."

"I'm on my way," he said.

When she put the phone down, she panicked. She had heard the smirk in his voice. He appeared to consider it a ruse to get him. After all his insults, what, in his mind, could be a better ploy. Trap him through his horses.

He appeared within minutes. He had hastily pulled on a pair of jeans and a loose black shirt which had tousled his hair. She had never seen him so casually dressed and it emphasised his panther-like qualities. He had such a loose-limbed elegance. He scowled at the sight of her which sent messages of fear flashing through her. Fortunately, he swiftly turned his attention to the stable and the horse.

"My God," was his reaction. "Get to his head and soothe him and keep clear of those legs." Iatro was still uselessly striving to fling his legs over to roll on his side, but he was so jammed between the wall and a bank of bedding, his efforts were futile.

"There's nothing for it. We'll have to rope him. He's too far over to manhandle." Drago disappeared for a rope as Morien tried to quieten the thrashing animal. Within minutes, he was back, tension contouring the lines of his body.

"Now," he instructed, "I want you to actually sit on his head to keep him still while I get the rope on him. Morien put her full weight on the frightened horse and tried to calm him. Drago roped the front legs and then reach for the rear. Iatro gave a mighty thrash almost cutting Drago's face.

"God," he sprang back "You're not heavy enough. Lean harder." Morien felt guilty and pressed herself down more firmly on Iatro's head whispering gently to him as Drago once more cautiously held a hind leg and quickly roped it. He just managed to avoid another searing blow and stood back. Morien could see the dark hair curling on his chest and was aware of the inherent strength in his muscled arms.

"Now, when I give the word, I want you to come over here and heave up the front legs whilst I heave the hinds. We wait for him to try by himself and then use his momentum to swing him over towards us. Whatever you do, keep clear of his legs. Now!"

Morien leapt up and grabbed the rope. Iatro thrashed but they mistimed the pull and Morien nearly ended up on top of the horse. She was rewarded with a scowl.

"Now again, and pull harder," snapped the Baron. Suddenly the horse rolled towards them, legs in all directions. There was a nasty moment when Drago released the thrashing legs and Iatro scrambled to his feet. Morien lost her balance and fell backwards. Drago pounced on her to pull her clear and she lay quivering in his arms. He held her very tightly as the trembling eased. She felt incredibly warm and secure. His lips brushed her forehead as he picked the straw out of her hair.

"Later my dear," he murmured. Embarrassed Morien released herself. How could she behave in a such a provocative manner? No wonder he was misinterpreting her. She went to the horse calming him while the Baron examined his legs and back for injuries.

"He seems all right. Lucky to get away with this." The Baron soothed the sweating horse. "Go and get a sweat scraper and a rug. We're going to have to walk him to dry him off." Morien ran to do his bidding. Between them they rubbed the animal down with scraper and straw and covered him with a light rug. It seemed so strange to be working so peacefully in tandem after all the earlier antagonism. They walked Iatro out into the starlight. Drago looked at her intently as though seeing her for the first time. After the earlier scene, there was a sense of unreality about strolling so peacefully in the warm night air. A mare and foal whickered as they passed down the drive. Morien shivered. For the first time, he spoke.

"Thank you for alerting me. How did you come to find Iatro?" he asked.

"I was saying goodnight to Merlin," she responded.

"Ah, yes. Your horse, tell me about him."

"There's not much to tell," said Morien cautiously. "He was bred by my father."

"Mmm?" the Baron encouraged.

Morien forced her tired brain into action. "Yes, we had several mares of good quality, but I had to sell them when my father died. Too expensive," she said off-handedly.

"Why did you keep the stallion?"

"He's too young for most of the buyers plus the fact that he's entire."

"Isn't he rather a handful?"

"Not really. He's been well treated and anyway he was my only legacy."

"More an encumbrance when you have to earn a living," commented the Baron. "What happened to your father?"

"He died recently in an accident." Morien turned her back on him not prepared to discuss the details. He seemed to get the message and let the matter drop. Let her keep her mysteries for now. She was obviously still raw on that subject unless she was an exceptional actress. They continued to walk, Morien

49

desperately aware of his closeness. The intensity of her feelings was so strong that she wondered at them, realising suddenly that despite his treatment of her, her body was still attracted to him even if her mind wasn't. This was all nonsense. After Gino, she had vowed that no man should touch her again. The mare called again.

"That's a lovely mare and foal, in fact they're all beautiful," said Morien inanely trying to get her mind away from this powerful man. "Is it usual for them to be out at night?"

"Yes, at this time of the year when the days are hot, and the flies are a nuisance. This was one of our best brood mares. She stamps her stock well."

"What does that mean? asked Morien conversationally

"She reproduces her good points in her foals. You may have noticed her paces, the way she floats? The foal has the same movement."

"Why did you say: she was?"

"Well, we are having trouble getting her in foal again this season. She has been to the stallion several times but doesn't hold. She missed at the foal heat and the second cycle when she came into season. We cannot seem to get her pregnant again. Hope there is no damage. We'll try again in a few weeks when she comes into season again, but it may be that we'll have to resort to IVF."

For some time, he expounded the economics of horse breeding. Morien was completely fascinated. On the subject of horses, he was totally alive. Eventually tiredness overtook her. Hiding a yawn, she stroked Iatro's coat. It was cool and dry. The Baron smiled.

"Yes, we can take him back now." At the stable door, the Baron paused glancing down at Morien, his eyes fixing on hers. For a moment, she thought he was going to give her a repeat performance of his earlier actions and she shied away. "I wonder what you're up to," he murmured, putting Iatro in the stable. As he closed the door, suddenly he turned to her and pulled her sharply towards him so that she fell against his chest.

"Perhaps we should go and find our own patch of straw," he said suggestively. Dreamily she looked into his eyes, too tired to argue any more. For a long time, they simply stared at one another, the warmth of their blended bodies uniting them.

"Too tired even to seduce me?" he smiled. She resisted then, trying to extricate herself. He let her go.

"Go now. I'll see to Iatro. You won't be fit for anything in the morning. Let alone now" he murmured to her retreating back.

CHAPTER 8

Morien was excessively tired when she got to bed that night with all the tension from the rescue and fear of making mistakes, she overslept. She was so late there was no time to sort out her new clothes. When she reached the yard, there was quite a buzz going on. Instead of working all the girls were standing around chatting, including Helen - surprise, surprise.

"Have you heard the Baron's girlfriend, Nina Blackthorpe-Smith, is here?" exclaimed Gill. "She arrived last night with the new intake. Quite a looker."

"No. I've only just made it down."

Helen was also scornful, saying uncharacteristically "I reckon she just wants to keep an eye on him. I can't see her getting her hands dirty." Everyone knew Helen wasn't looking forward to Nina's arrival. Up till now, Nina tended to drop in unexpectedly looking for the Baron and they'd never really got on well. From what was being said, Morien could see that the standard yard discipline could be compromised.

"You're right there," agreed Gill "Gossip has it that her father is a VIP on the Council and that the boss is only taking her on because he's angling for planning permission to put up another indoor school."

"You'd do well not to talk of that," reprimanded Helen gently.

"Can't he just do that anyway?" asked Morien

"No, no. All this property is listed, that is it's ancient and comes under the jurisdiction of English Heritage. You have to get permission to make any sort of alteration – plus the fact that it's green belt. It seems an indoor school doesn't qualify here as a farm building." This was all utterly mysterious to Morien who'd never lived in a permanent building, so she just nodded wisely.

"He plays his cards close, so I don't think she is aware of any of that," said Helen

"Who, Nina?"

"Yes. If she's just looking for a husband how on earth will I cope with her?"

"You will treat her like any other student," said an icy voice. There he was within feet of them, so elegant in his long riding coat. "Stop gossiping, there's work to be done."

So unfortunately caught in the act, Helen looked very upset as the girls watched his angry receding back. "It's not fair how he creeps up on us." exclaimed Gill.

"Well get back to work as he demanded," said Helen "Let's have some discipline around here, especially since here she comes." All the girls eyed Nina surreptitiously as Helen greeted her. She was quite something - tall, dark, clear-skinned, immaculate. She had an air of confidence not the usual nervousness of a new student.

"Well," thought Morien as she watched Helen introduce the newcomer to the mysteries of the establishment, "At least I won't have to fraternise with her". She recognised immediately that there was a pecking order, and this new girl was not about to step over its boundaries. It appeared to Morien that there were advantages in being a WP. She didn't have to mix with the snobs in her unsuitable clothes, which she was still wearing for mucking out and stable work.

Gill had briefed her about Nina who had been to the stables on many occasions in the past. It seems she had first come as a child, obsessed with ponies, learning to ride and join in all the gymkhanas and other activities arranged for the clients. She had progressed to show ponies when her father had bought her an extremely expensive and highly successful "school master" show pony on which she became a well-known winner locally.

"I gather she used to keep her ponies here. Then she discovered show jumping and Daddy again obliged by buying her an experienced and reliable animal which they kept at home until it was retired. I'm told she did badly at school and being without an aim and had started to develop a reputation for being somewhat wild."

"She certainly seems to have had all the advantages," said Morien

"I expect Daddy had decided that training towards a qualification to work with horses would keep her out of mischief."

Morien covertly watched as Nina listened to Helen and she was clearly not impressed.

53

She heard Nina say "Surely I'm not expected to get my hands dirty. With my experience am I not let off such duties?"

"You are registered for the training course, and all this is part of it," responded Helen.

"I'll have to have a word with Drago. After all I am almost as successful a competitor in my jumping field as he is in his."

She could just be heard muttering "At least the compensation was I'll see more of Drago. Why, oh why, had Daddy insisted on this? At home grooms do the dirty work. I just turn up and ride. I suppose I'd better look interested in the meantime," she turned her attention to Helen again.

"Six whole months of hard labour, combined with having to mix with the hoypaloi."

Morien could see that deep inside she was very unhappy.

As Helen took Nina off to the office, Morien went over to check the "orders of the day". To her amazement she found she had been given charge of the Baron's two specials, Iatro and Crystabelle, although her lessons would continue on Whisper. This was quite an up-grade, so her performance last night must have been understood and appreciated. As the Baron had already exercised Iatro, fortunately there could not have been any aftereffects.

Care of Puffin and Whisper had been relegated to the new intake. They were obviously test horses that were used to teach students how to handle awkwardness. This was quite a relief for Morien. She liked them as characters but not riding Puffin nor his endless habit of biting and bucking. She felt that both horses had combined in a conspiracy especially to show her up on her lessons, although Whisper could go well if not distracted. Both Helen and the Baron nagged her unmercifully - keep your legs back, sit up, keep the rein contact, make him dance a little. Why couldn't they pick on someone else in the group? It was always "Morien this and Morien that" until she felt as though she was the only one there.

Yesterday she had risked wearing her new boots in the hope that she would have more control, but it was a disastrous session. The first half had been jumping and Whisper had run out consistently. She thought she was going to dream "rein contact! rein contact!" Jumping was silly anyway. The horse appeared to think so too. Morien really only wanted to float and dance. Then that part of the lesson had been spoiled by Whisper panicking every time she passed the gallery. A client had been watching the lesson and kept flapping a piece of paper, ostensibly to cool herself. Morien was really mad because she knew she could have performed well without all the nagging and distraction. It made her tense, and this communicated itself to her horse.

"I'm so fed up I'm going to give all this up," she confided in Gill as she stabled the horse.

"Hey, not so fast," exclaimed Gill "What's got into you?"

"I'm utterly sick to death of all this criticism. Nag, nag, nag, nag! No one ever says a word of encouragement. I feel like a useless sack of potatoes."

"You don't realise how lucky you are," said Gill enviously

"What on earth do you mean? What's lucky about going through that torture every day?"

"What you're too stupid to realise," said Gill "is that it's because you're good that you get all the nagging. If you're no use, like me, they don't take any notice of you. Sometimes, I go through a whole lesson without a word from them."

"Oh Gill," said Morien, chastened "You know you're not a bad rider. You're a much better jumper than me."

"That may be. But who's interested in jumpers here? So just you shut up and thank your lucky stars." Gill brushed her eyes as she marched into the stable. Well, thought Morien, they certainly have a funny way of telling you you're any use. It was food for thought. Perhaps she could find a way to help Gill. The talent was there but hid itself away under scrutiny during lessons.

For the next week, she worked flat out, determined that the Baron should never have cause to complain about his horses. One of the benefits was that she was going to be allowed to ride Crystabelle occasionally for lessons. Also now the Baron had his special pupil, Nina, to claim his attention. She seemed an excellent rider, but with her main interest being in show jumping than the Baron's first love of dressage, how long would she survive. Morien felt this would not do her much good here as she remembered Gill's comments about the attitude to jumping - merely a necessary evil for examination purposes.

Nina had a dramatic personality enhanced by her dark hair and slightly olive skin, which set off her aquiline features. Her voluptuous figure had a hard fitness about it. From the start, it was fairly clear to the other students that she did not intend to learn anything, let alone work. Whenever she could get away with it, she saddled up and went show jumping in the outdoor ménage for an hour or two a day. Then if the Baron was around, she appeared wherever he was working ostensibly to "learn from watching". If he was out or away, she simply disappeared back to her room for the rest of the time. Helen had been exasperated at first but had finally given up It was obvious, even to the blind, that Nina had set her cap at the Baron, and everyone appeared to feel that it would be a good match - the two autocrats were made for each other.

Nina could hardly deign to speak to the W.P.s except to treat them as grooms and consequently made herself very unpopular. She was also very resentful of Morien's position in charge of the Baron's special horses. Since her arrival, she had taken to coming into the two loose boxes to give them the once-over – on behalf of the Baron, of course. This meant that there was a subtle war going on and she never lost a chance to put Morien down - always with a sweet smile on her face.

"Ah Morien," she said as she poked her head around the door of Iatro's loose box. "I see that you have remembered to skip out regularly. Have you picked out Iatro's feet?"

"Naturally," responded Morien. "And I've changed the water buckets, cleaned the manger, and groomed him down." Morien hoped her sarcastic responses would do the trick, but no, Nina seemed immune. It was all deliberately toned to create a mistress/servant relationship.

"Of course, you realise that any detail overlooked could cause a setback in his training and there is this important milestone on the horizon." Morien could hardly believe her ears. Anyway, why wasn't Nina attending to her own duties instead of hassling her? Especially as it was clear that as far as Nina was concerned when she married Drago she wouldn't bother with the yard. She would be too busy entertaining and travelling to take more than an occasional ride.

As the days passed, Morien found that she was in conflict with Nina even though, wherever possible she avoided her. Regrettably, from time to time the WPs and paying students trained together. During these group lessons Nina somehow impeded Morien. She always seemed to be in the way, giving the impression that Morien wasn't paying sufficient attention. How did she manage it?

Today was particularly bad. Nina constantly manoeuvred herself in front of Morien, would slow the pace or go slightly off-track causing Morien to check. Repeatedly she managed to cut across, bump against her or baulk her horse thus spoiling the animal's stride.

"God, here she comes again. Come one, Puffin, stretch a little and we'll get around her." Nina was so subtle that it always appeared to be Morien's fault.

"She's at it again. It's not fair, we're upsetting the paces of all the others." Even if Morien circled always Nina followed suit placing herself once more in front. She seemed to do everything she could to discredit her and make her appear ignorant and incompetent.

"I'm not going to get mad," thought Morien refusing to rise. "She's so childish."

Whenever she could, she kept out of the way especially if it was a jumping session since Nina so obviously excelled in that area, but try as she might, Nina stuck to her like glue.

Today they'd had a horrid session in the jumping arena when Morien's horse had constantly run out and refused to jump while Nina, having cleared everything with ease, sat and gloated. She kept commenting to Helen on the low standard of the working pupils and hillbillies and wondered loudly how the Baron could have possibly taken them on for training.

CHAPTER 9

As last the session ended and, for the first time in ages, Morien had a spare hour plus her lunch break. She had delayed her ride on Merlin until now. It was just the therapy she needed; she was so exasperated. She had found a secluded spot on the far side of the woods where she'd been working at his training unobserved. Now that she'd been here almost a month, she felt that what she did was so unorthodox that it didn't need publicising and could understand the Earl's reservations about her background in circus training.

Although he was young, Merlin was remarkably well balanced, and he had reached the normally very difficult paces of passage and piaffe. To her delight he seemed to enjoy these movements and show off. Riding bareback, Morien was able to communicate precisely through her weight shifts and thus keep a completely still leg. This was why she found all the "leg aids" she was being taught so difficult. Even more so when she discovered that, with a little persuasion, all the school horses, even Puffin, responded to her slight weight changes quite readily.

Each day Merlin's paces improved. He sidestepped from the lightest indication and floated daintily despite his size. It never entered Morien's head that he was very advanced for his age, although her father had always said that he reckoned Merlin to be the best potential he had ever had. She trained him in her father's tradition where such progress was the norm.

She did have one problem, however, with his flying changes, the skipping canter. She did need the help of a ground jockey, someone on the ground watching the timing of her instructions and the responses of horse's legs. As if in answer to her prayer Merlin nickered and, looking up she saw Nathan and Rankin. What was quite delightful was that they were both on horseback. She trotted over. "So, you've been persevering." she exclaimed leaning across and kissing Nathan on his cheek.

"Yes," he smiled happily. "I realised when you mentioned riding that it had been in the back of my mind for some time because in the summer, I get tired of touring the estate in the Land Rover. After a few sessions with the disabled class down at the stables, I found it was such fun and now they let me out on my own - with Rankin that is. Also, it enables me to reach areas of the estate that were totally unsuitable even for a four-wheel drive."

"We saw you coming this way, miss and his Lordship was adamant to follow and see if you were schooling." Rankin looked really important.

"Yes, no one disturbs me here. I don't think what I'm doing would merit general approval," she laughed.

"We guessed when we discovered the riding ring you have created. It was several weeks ago when I was checking all the woodlands." Morien looked aghast. "It's all right," Nathan reassured her, "my son doesn't come this way. He just beats a track from stable to indoor school and back again. He's simply no idea what he's missing out here in the open air. Show me how Merlin's getting on." Morien was delighted.

Merlin was on form and was a real show-off anyway. He loved an audience so excelled, particularly in the passage. Nathan watched as the big stallion literally danced beneath the trees, dappled by the sunlight. "What a picture. She resembles a sylph-like centaur." he murmured to Rankin.

Morien finished the performance with one-time changes approaching the Earl. Once again, she had trouble, so did a pirouette and came to a halt in front of him. "Marvellous." he exclaimed glowingly.

"Yes, until the end," said Morien "I simply can't get the rhythm right at the moment. I just can't feel what is going wrong."

"You want some help?"

"Yes."

"When do you usually come out?"

"Oh, 5.30 in the morning, before I go to work, except on my day's off, that is."

Nathan looked at her and shook his head. "Such dedication. I wonder you have the energy to carry on. Well we'll have to see what we can do."

"You mean you'll come out at that time?"

"I'm not promising anything, but I'll try."

"I could practise that bit during my lunch hour. That would be more practical, wouldn't it?"

"You must eat, child," scolded the Earl

"Well, we don't have to do it every day. You could guide me and then I could practise what I've learnt in the mornings on my own."

"It's a deal," laughed the Earl

All three made their way back to the yard together. As they arrived, surprise, surprise Nina suddenly materialised, all solicitous, to help the Earl. She firmly turned her back on Morien. While he graciously accepted her attentions, Morien disappeared into Merlin's box to rub him down. A little later Nina put her head over the door. "You really should keep that brute of yours away from the Earl when he's riding. It's dangerous and Nathan cannot afford to have another accident.

Morien looked startled. "He wouldn't hurt a fly," she said.

"There's always a first time. Stallions are notoriously unreliable. Have you no imagination?" The picture of Merlin panicking and killing her father flashed into Morien's mind. Perhaps Nina had a point. She would have to be careful. It would never do to let her know, so she just gave her a "sweet" smile. However, the hidden truth had hurt.

With Merlin settled, she went in to deal with her other charges. There was something odd about Iatro's box which she couldn't immediately identify. Then she noticed that the water buckets were soiled by dirty straw. In fact, the stable was quite a mess. "What's up, Iatro?" she asked giving him a friendly shove. "You been doing the highland fling?" She set about tidying up the mess, rinsing out the buckets and adjusting Iatro's rugs.

In Crystabelle's box she found a similar mess. "Hi Crystabelle, how'd you get that stuff in your bucket? Did something frighten you?" She caressed the horse who nuzzled her. As she refreshed the stable and set fair her mind kept going back to Nina's words. Would Merlin misbehave again? He'd had a good excuse at the circus. What might frighten him here? She'd have to be more careful.

She began wondering what had upset the Baron's horses. They both seemed normal, bright eyed with no obvious injuries. She decided to pop in on them at intervals for the rest of the day to ensure that they were not sickening for something. Fortunately, all remained calm, which was a relief because, as she bedded them down for the night.

To Morien's dismay the next day disaster struck again. She'd only been away for her lunch hour schooling Merlin. What on earth had led to such a change in behaviour? After lunch was normally the quietest time in the yard. With everyone elsewhere the horses that were not working usually dozed peacefully. Yet for the last 3 days her two charges seemed under stress during the afternoons. They didn't have temperatures; their eyes were clear yet both boxes were absolutely saturated.

Once more, she had to empty them completely and re-lay the beds. Well, at least with no lessons she would be able to watch the two animals and discover what was happening at this crucial time of day. She settled herself down with a book. Once she thought she heard footsteps but apart from that all was quiet.

Nothing happened for the rest of that day and the early part of the next. The horses were quite calm and didn't appear to be sick. So, on the third day Morien took Merlin out for a stretch. She felt oppressed and depressed, needed to blow away the misery. The Baron was treating her as though she didn't exist. She might just as well be a piece of the furniture. When he did catch her eye, his eyes glittered dangerously and she retreated into her shell of anonymity. She was beginning to realise that her moods related to whether she saw the Baron or not. She admitted bleakly that he was the highlight of her day and just seeing him sent flashes of fire to the pit of her stomach. It shocked her as she realised that on one level she was always alert for sounds of him in the yard. Her senses were so acute that she knew when he was approaching. She warred with herself - one part wanting to throw itself at his feet and the other wanting to give him a piece of her mind. But when he was in the same space all this was over-ridden by a mad desire for the strength and comfort of his arms around her.

"I'm like some idiot in a romantic novel." she thought crossly. "How can my body long for his touch when my mind hates him, fears him even?" She urged Merlin on and encouraged him to stretch and stretch, hoping the exertion would have a cathartic effect on her emotions.

Breathless they arrived at the farthest boundary of the estate, where it rose towards the downs, a part she had not explored before. Morien realised that she could see the sea, blue, peaceful and sparkling. She recalled memories of her father, of splashing and swimming the horses to keep their legs in good trim. She closed her eyes and could almost feel the water and the strong motion of the swimming horse.

"Nothing like salt water," he used to say. "Takes down any swelling and heals as well." She remembered whenever they pitched near the sea, he advocated swimming to keep muscles in trim, especially when horses were off work for any reason. "If you're ever near the sea, take them in." he used to say. "The change of scenery, the space, the healing qualities of mind and body are just what a circus horse needs."

Images of her father flowed through her mind. She seemed to have come a long way since she left the circus. The complete change of lifestyle had been hard at first. For the other girls, it was simply a change of house but for her, who had never been static, who loved the variety in the scenery as they travelled, the constantly changing faces, the excitement of arriving at a new venue, so much of it had been quite alien. This massive change combined with the loss of her father was almost like emigrating. Merlin cropped the grass and Morien felt sun-warmed and at peace, the Baron temporarily forgotten. She listened to the sounds around her – the distant ripple of the sea, the low hum of insects in the grass and the gentle summer perfumes pervading the air. Eventually her reverie was broken by the distant chiming of the clock carrying on the gentle breeze. Work constantly nagged and she reluctantly retraced her steps.

On her return, she looked in on the other two horses before going for tea. To her horror, once more the boxes were a sodden mess. This time someone had lodged the brick of salt lick against the valve in the drinking trough so that the water constantly flowed. Morien stood aghast. Then something niggled in her mind. Why had she been so blind? It always happened when she was elsewhere and there appeared to be nothing amiss with the horses. It was blatantly obvious that someone was getting at her. Her mind completely suspicious, she went to check the "orders for the day" to see who was not occupied during the time she had been away. Monica Scott, Elizabeth Thompson, Jeremy Wills, Pauline Foster, Sue Mackintosh, Nina Blackthorpe-Smith, Peter Pilsner, Freddie Storn. There were really too many, and of course, each day the group changed. The only possibility was Nina since Morien knew she was jealous although she couldn't think why because there was no way Nina wanted to get her hands dirty. However, she was spiteful. Morien decided to watch her fellow grooms unobtrusively to try to find a common denominator. But why would any of them do such a thing? Perhaps she was just being paranoid. She thought of confiding in Gill but there was really so little to go on. It was only instinct that made her suspect Nina. She set about clearing up the mess.

Again, Helen caught her at it. "Look here, we simply can't have you wasting all this straw," she said. "How many bales have you got through this week?" Morien did not answer. "One more incident like this and I'll dock it off your wages."

Morien was speechless. She couldn't watch them 24 hours a day. It was all so unfair. She was trapped trapped. There was nowhere to run. Weeping silently, she acknowledged that there was no alternative. She remembered that it was her evening off and decided to take herself off to the village and talk to some perfectly ordinary people. Let whoever was messing her about do their damnedest. Life couldn't get any worse.

CHAPTER 10

It was latish when she eventually escaped. Gill lent her a bicycle and as she rode through the gates, she felt like an uncaged bird. She wound her way through the lanes to a small cluster of cottages and there was assailed by the delicious aroma of fish and chips. Perfect, she could just about afford the luxury and why not indulge herself for once. She joined the small queue.

"They've let you out, have they?" laughed an elderly man. Morien looked non-plussed. "I beg your pardon."

"Well, you must be from the Hall, starving and out on your own," he laughed again. Morien now laughed with him. "Gosh, is that how you see us?"

"Don't they feed you up there?"

"Yes, but I needed a change." Something shadowed her eyes. The man noticed and turned away.

It was her turn. "Cod and chips, please" She noticed the woman piling extra chips into the bag. The woman smiled and said, "Got to get your skin off your bones, young lady."

The food smelt delicious, and Morien found a bench overlooking the pond. She ate greedily with greasy fingers. There were some youths larking about outside the shop with loud ribald laughter. Someone shouted at them, and they pushed off mouthing obscenities. Morien was relieved as the peace returned. An enquiring swan floated near the bank and sparrows pecked around her feet. She stretched, replete and closed her eyes trying to make the moment last.

Once more the handsome Drago flashed into her mind. She studied her emotional responses. Was she really afraid of him? In her heart, she knew she was not. Her desire was overwhelming. She didn't know how to handle this magnetic feeling whenever she was in his presence. She wanted him, almost to be inside his skin. Was she falling in love, in love with a man who appeared to dislike everything about her, a man who would hate her completely when he knew her background? It was dreadful to be so naïve. She needed someone to talk to. She had never had the guidance of a mother or even another woman or girl of her own age. There was certainly no one in her present environment in whom she could confide. Certainly, not Gill or even Helen and Nathan who had become a surrogate father would probably be horrified.

Her mind wandered. Visions of a family life that she'd never had – the loneliness of her father suddenly made sense. Although he was good to her, he spent more time with the horses who gave him unconditional love, she supposed.

Eventually, the nagging thoughts of the 5.30 a.m. start took over. The light had left the pond and given way to twilight. The many birds were flying to their roosting places. Lethargically, Morien strolled back to her bike where, horror of horrors, the louts had let down both tyres. She had no bicycle pump. No one in the chip shop could help her, so there was nothing for it but to start the long walk back. "Seems I just can't win." she sighed disconsolately as she trudged up the hill. When at last the gates came into view it was getting quite dark.

Headlights lit the road behind her, so she moved close to the gateposts. As the vehicle came alongside it stopped. "Inevitable" she thought "it had to be the Baron." He ran down the window and scowled at her.

"You. I might have known. No lights, no reflective clothing. Don't you know it's illegal?"

"I was walking," protested Morien

"So I noticed. Why?"

"None of your business," said Morien wearily, no longer caring what he thought of her.

"It is my business. I want my horses properly cared for, which means their groom should not be gallivanting about at night in the dark, putting herself at risk." He got out of the car and came around to her. "And you're not doing a very good job at present." She backed off behind the bicycle like a frightened animal. Drago hesitated. She could almost read his thoughts. There was a sense that he wanted to look after her and yet beat her at the same time? She saw him checking the bike and registering the flat tyres and lack of pump. Without a word, he took it out of her nerveless hands and put it into the back of the Land Rover. Then he opened the passenger door.

"Get in," he commanded. She did not move. Irritated he said "You have my word that I will not touch you. I merely have the interests of my horses at heart and wish to deliver you safely back to the yard." She got in and huddled tightly against the closed

65

door. Drago gave her a tight mirthless smile as he normally, he had a way with nervous creatures but supposed it was his own fault that this one was afraid. He appeared momentarily to have forgotten that she was supposed to be a brazen hussy. He drove right up to the hostel wing and she leapt out the moment the Land Rover stopped, only waiting for him to unload the bike. The urge for him to take her in his arms nearly overwhelmed her as she watched him warily, waiting for the bike. He held onto it. "Well?" he waited. She didn't move.

"Come here," he murmured softly and through all her tension and tiredness her self-control evaporated. Tears began to spill down her cheeks. He slipped an arm around her and held her close whilst she wept unashamedly into his jacket. The bitter sweetness of it was intoxicating.

Then she pulled away from a security which she knew was wrong. He was not her father, and the tingling passion was again rearing its head. He drew her back. She could feel the hardness of him against her hip and flames surged to her throat as he began searching for her lips.

"No," she cried shivering like a frightened doe. He held her wrist.

"But you want me as much as I want you. Why so prudish all of a sudden?"

She tried to draw on scorn that she did not feel. "I'll not be yet another addition to your list of conquests. Find someone more willing." He wrenched her back against him. "Like Nina She can hardly wait."

"Bitch. Think too much of yourself, don't you? My father's pet. I guess he's a wealthier catch."

"How dare you insult your father so. He's a better man than you."

"Better lover, do you mean?" She squirmed in his grasp. "With his background what can you expect. a sawdust traveller. Pah!" Morien felt cold to her very soul and backed away from him.

"Be kind enough to leave the bike. I am going to the yard for a final check." She turned on her heel and marched off with as much dignity as she could muster. Drago frowned after her, laughing at the minuscule indignant figure departing crowned with the last word.

She had decided that tomorrow she would throw caution to the winds and venture out in her new clothes as she was due for an individual lesson. She didn't want any carelessness to antagonise the Baron now when things were beginning to improve. The very thought was thrilling

"Just you wait, Nina. Now you'll have some real competition. Those clothes are as good as yours." she laughed to herself. "Gosh I'm just waiting to see her face and his. They suited each other really, both impressed by superficial appearances, never looking beyond.

The time had come. She scampered to her room and changed into her new outfit. "Just look at you!" she addressed the mirror. The jodhpurs fitted close to her leg, so she was able to pull the glossy black boots over them. No need for braces today she thought as she fastened the waist. She turned this way and that admiring herself in the mirror, her slimness and the perfect fit. She struggled a few times with the tie. Gosh, how do you fiddle this thing? So silly not to have done such simple things before. Who wore ties at the circus, she reminisced to herself? Only the clowns and they were enormous things that strung around the neck with elastic. She laughed at the memory. Perhaps she'd fix hers on a string. Drago's astonished face flashed in her mind.

"There now. Renaldo would be proud of me." she did a twirl as she fastened the jacket and snatched up the black jockey cap. "Oops, can't see." It was a trifle large but why worry. All the girls seemed to wear them down on their noses, but an image of the Baron came to her and so she found some tissues to stuff in the lining. It was a bit better, but she needed a hairnet not a ponytail. Ah well I'll have to do. She ran to the stables. Despite her caring for Iatro and Crystabelle she was not allowed to ride them yet, so she tacked up Whisper and made her way, full of anticipation to the indoor school. Maybe he wouldn't find so much fault with her today.

In the proper clothes, she knew she looked a million dollars, so different from the scruffy teenage appearance of her normal gear. The perfect fit of the clothes hugged her body highlighting its perfection. Helen raised an eyebrow. "Your trunk arrived then?" she enquired eyeing her up and down. Morien made a non-committal noise and took off around the school on Whisper. Where was Drago? She realised that her legs wrapped around the horse much better with proper boots. The wellies had been too short and had kept catching on the saddle flaps. Every now and then she caught sight of herself in the long mirrors at the end of the school and felt really proud. She imagined how smart, how absolutely right she would look riding beside the Baron. Even Whisper seemed to be on her best behaviour.

"Pay attention," called Helen bringing her out of her reverie. "I do believe you're not listening," she said in exasperation. "Quit admiring yourself. Your new clothes have gone right to your head." Morien looked suitably admonished.

Everything about the session had been exceptional from her appearance to her performance but the Baron wasn't there. She was incredibly disappointed that he hadn't come, even felt a little let down which made her realise how much she wanted his admiration - his approval.

"I must snap out of this" she thought as she put Whisper away and went to check her charges. At the boxes of Iatro and Crystabelle, her elegant appearance became irrelevant. She found the Baron in Iatro's box. He looked stormy. "What is this mess?" he ranted. Morien looked in dismay - complete disorder.

"I don't know," she stuttered.

"You don't know, you don't know," he taunted "I want the best for my horses and this will NOT do." He eyed her with fury. "I must have been out of my mind when I gave you the responsibility for them. Three o'clock in the afternoon and the morning mucking-out not even started. And there are you all dressed up in your fancy clothes like a paying client. Who do you think you are? The horses, that is WORK, the first priority here."

Morien was completely dismayed. How could Iatro make such a mess? It almost looked as if someone had used his stable as the muckheap and dumped barrow loads of manure in it.

As he towered over her. Morien longed to stand up for herself, to put him on alert that she had no control over the situation. But what was the point. He wouldn't believe her, his opinion of her was so low. It galled her to think that she cared that he should see her in her new clothes. How incredibly childish, how naïve.

68

When was she going to learn that she meant nothing to him, that she was simply a WP lucky to have a roof over her head? It seemed that she was constantly divorced her feelings for him from his attitude towards her? With a final scowl, he turned sharply, and she backed away from him feeling that he would rip the jacket from her back.

"You are removed from lessons for the next week to ensure that the standard of these boxes is pristine." He all but slammed the stable door behind him. Morien was shattered especially when she heard the expostulations coming from Crystabelle's box next door. As he finally walked away Drago was perplexed. Did she really set out to anger him? She had looked fantastic in her new clothes, and he would have liked to tell her so. But the mess!! In this place horses always come first, and that little slut had let glamour go to her head. Perhaps he'd made a mistake – he should get another groom for Iatro and Crystabelle.

Morien set about clearing up. She was so angry that she began to think that life with Gino in the circus might just have been a better deal. The whole situation was beyond her comprehension but as she worked, she remembered that this had happened on a lesser scale yesterday. It took her the rest of the day because to make it perfect she needed to completely empty the stable and start the deep litter beds all over again.

Helen put her head over the door. "What's this I hear? Are you letting the side down? I can't go on championing you forever," she said disparagingly "Just because you now look the part, you shouldn't let it go to your head, like some people we know." The jibe was not lost on Morien. Fancy comparing her with Nina Blackthorpe-Smith.

The image of the angry Baron haunted Morien. It seemed that no matter what she did she could not please him. She now realised that she'd wanted so much to impress him and merit his approval. Treacherous thoughts. To think that she had been delighted to be entrusted with his "specials". Honoured, in fact, thinking that he was seeing her at last as a good WP, that she was worthy of his trust. Well, he could go and take a jump because if she couldn't have lessons, she would spend more time with Merlin. Nathan had been as good as his word, sneaking out unobserved a couple of times a week to help her during her lunch break. At least he was appreciative of her and her horse.

CHAPTER 12

Morien went to see Merlin who was munching hay looking placid and content. She blew him a kiss and he blew back. Crystabelle was also peaceful. Finally, she let herself into Iatro's box. Horror of horrors. He was standing on three legs. One of his forelegs was tangled in his hay net which was hanging at floor level.

Morien could not believe her eyes. She had learnt at a very early age about hanging hay nets and the dangers of horses becoming entangled. It was absolutely basic. She always hung them high attaching them with a horse proof safety knot. There was no way Iatro could have lowered it alone. She checked the knot and found it has been re-tied with a simple slip knot. Now she knew it was sabotage. There was absolutely no way she could have tied it like that, even if she had been in a daydream.

She struggled to loosen the slipped and tightened knot and gently disentangled Iatro's leg, putting the net out of the door. The back of his fetlock was raw where he had been thrashing to release himself. Already the joint was beginning to swell. The pain must have been intense.

As she went to boil water and find dressings, she rang Helen. The matter had to be reported. Although she knew what to do, here she was only a W.P. Helen arrived as Morien had all the vetinerary stuff together. She said nothing. The pain on Morien's face said it all. Silently they worked on the injury bound it for the night and settled the horse down. Helen re-hung the hay net - a gesture not lost on Morien. They returned to the office. They sat opposite each other while Helen decided where to begin.

"It is noticeable," she said at last "that it is not your horse that is neglected." Morien paled.

"Whilst Iatro and Crystabelle's boxes are in turmoil, Merlin lives in paradise." Morien opened her mouth but was silenced.

"Whatever special circumstances have brought you and your horse here, I am not party to. However, the care of all the animals is my responsibility and if this casual attitude continues, you and your horse will have to go or else he will have to be cut and turned out with the other geldings. Do you understand me?"

"Yes," whispered Morien. In her anxiety and frustration, she had never conceived this sinister aspect to the situation. Castrated and put out to grass. Her Merlin. It was unthinkable.

"Have you anything to say?"

"Only that things go wrong the minute I turn my back."

"Then you had better not turn your back and put a proper effort into the job." Helen warned. "Now go to bed."

"What about telling the Baron?" Morien blurted.

"I'll do that," said Helen, after all it's my job she thought. A picture of utter dejection, Morien made her way to bed. Things were beginning to form a pattern in her mind. Since the attacks seemed to be concentrated on Iatro and Crystabelle, was she really the butt or was someone trying to get at the Baron, trying to prevent his success, destroy his reputation? She simply couldn't understand how anyone could hurt the horses whatever their motives. What kind of mentality was that? Callous in the extreme, the sort of person who cared little for sensitivity or pain be it man or beast. She wondered who had been on duty that evening. She was determined to find out in the morning.

First thing, knowing Helen would be exercising her charges in the indoor school for at least another 20 minutes, Morien slipped into the office and searched for the duplicate copies of the "Orders for the Day". Who had been on duty last night? She ran her finger through the lists - aha. There it was - Nina Blackthorpe-Smith. She then examined the previous days when she had been out of the yard and on each occasion Nina's name was amongst those responsible for the yard activities at those times. Could it possibly be her? She had been very catty about the messy stables. All pretty damming, but still she had no proof. She wondered about confronting her but what could she say. It was all speculation and Nina was so snotty that one couldn't have a conversation with her anyway.

In the days that followed Morien was relieved of any duties caring for Iatro and Crystabelle. The Baron had been preparing Iatro for a major competition in 6 weeks' time and now with this massive interruption, it was unlikely the horse would be ready. What made matters worse was that overnight there had been a major setback in the healing process as Iatro had been allergic to the vet's treatment. Morien watched him day and night, even secretly sleeping in the stable. Not that there was now any point

71

in continuing to discredit her. She couldn't have been any lower in the Baron's estimation.

The Baron was bemoaning the delay and the way Iatro was losing his working muscles through inactivity. He treated Morien as though she wasn't there, always talking over her head to Helen.

With her disgrace preventing her from participating in anything but caring for Iatro, Morien spent more time with Merlin. One thing he enjoyed was loose schooling which Morien found she could do in the outdoor school since she still had a clear view of Iatro's stable. Merlin could safely run free in the wooden fenced area of the school, and he loved to play, rearing up and leaping about like a spring lamb when first let out. After five minutes or so of sport, however, he would settle and listen to Morien's voice understanding her commands and responding like a sheep dog. He would turn to left or right, walk, trot or canter, stop, start and even jump a small fence. In this way, a lot of exercise could be crammed into a short time and Morien had a chance to examine his paces from the ground. Gill and the other girls often came to watch amazed at his docility and obedience. On one occasion Morien let Gill have a go. She was enthralled once she managed to imitate Morien's voice commands and Merlin obliged.

One day, after a particularly good session with Merlin, Morien decided to stop being a mouse and retrieve credibility. She was in the loosebox when Drago came in to examine Iatro yet again and complained, she said "I'd like to make a suggestion."

"What makes you think I'd want to listen?" he responded scathingly

"Because I know it works," said Morien boldly

"Well."

"Whenever we were near the sea and had horses with leg trouble, my father and I used to swim them." The Baron looked interested "Go on." he said.

"The advantage is that the sea water helped to heal the wound or swelling, and the swimming keeps up the muscle. The sea is near enough and the beach is level."

"Yes, I've heard of this treatment for racehorses but thought of it only taking place in special swimming pools." He stood musing for a moment. "I suppose we could box him over to the coast. It may be sensible to take a second horse the first time."

"I could bring Merlin." Morien said hastily. "He loves the sea and would be a good lead if Iatro is afraid."

"Afraid?"

"They often are when they see the sea and breaking waves for the first time."

"Well, little Miss Know-all, I am prepared to try anything now. No time like the present."

"We'll need webbing bridles, because the sea water will spoil leather," reminded Morien.

"Organise something with Helen."

Helen was startled at the plan but after much searching managed to put together two bridles out of webbing head collars and reins. Then Morien dashed back to the house and put on her swimming costume under her jodhpurs.

The Baron brought the horsebox around and suitably decked for travelling, both horses were ready for loading. Morien noticed a towel on the driver's seat. Would he strip off she wondered as unbidden a vision flashed through her mind's eye.

"I need another pair of hands, Helen. Organise me a groom please."

To Morien's utter dismay, Nina appeared, immaculate as ever. She always seemed to be lurking when the Baron was in the yard. She chatted amiably with the Baron leaving Morien to do the groom's work, the job Nina had just been asked to do - loading the horses, checking the lorry was fastened safely and all the other little chores. Ostentatiously she climbed up in front with the Baron. Although there was room for three in the cab, Morien decided the back with Iatro for the journey was more comfortable for more reasons than one.

CHAPTER 13

At the beach, Iatro was sorted out first. Morien did not want Nina touching Merlin. She needn't have worried as Nina flirted and drooled as she removed Iatro's travelling gear. The Baron seemed impervious and then took himself off to the groom's compartment to change. Morien removed all Merlin's travelling gear, then hiding behind the horse she slipped off her jodhpurs, retaining her T-shirt for modesty and led the horse down the ramp.

When the Baron emerged in swimming trunks and shirt, Nina practically ate him up. She was so obvious, it was embarrassing. But, Morien had trouble keeping her eyes off him too. He was magnificent, a perfect physique, broad shouldered. The elegant triangular shape of muscled torso tapering to slim hips and long, lithe legs. She noticed he had beautiful hands and feet. He had loosely tied his shirt at the waist revealing just the right amount of dark hair curling down his chest, disappearing suggestively into blue trunks. She turned away; her breath held so tightly she almost choked.

"Better keep those leather boots out of the salt, Nina," called the Baron as she gave him a leg up onto Iatro's back. Nina smirked and ogled at him.

Morien missed the look in his eyes as she vaulted lightly onto Merlin and brought him to hand. Never had he seen any of the pupils, or staff for that matter, vault so easily. Who was this girl? Bareback they walked the horses to the water's edge and Merlin started to prance.

"Steady boy, steady there. We've got to look after Iatro." And Drago, thought Drago to himself as he suddenly felt a trifle apprehensive. Thoughts of Quentin flashed into his mind. Iatro was not that keen as the wavelets broke on the shore and kept shying away. Merlin, however, pranced gaily forward and was soon up to his belly. When Morien realised Iatro's reluctance, she came back and quite naturally took hold of the bridle leading him gently into the water. For the first time in a very long time, the Baron felt inadequate as his attention was elsewhere.

74

Once over the breaking edge, Iatro relaxed, and the companionable duo walked knee deep along the shore. The silence between them however became more and more intense.

"When walking like this the drag of the water needs effort and helps to strengthen their muscles, " said Morien, trying to be conversational.

"That makes sense. Your father was a sensible man. What sort of injuries did he have to deal with?" asked Drago probingly.

"Oh occasional, muscular pulls, reducing swelling if the horses had had to travel for a long time, or had an injury - sometimes a pricked or bruised sole. It helps to draw out any festering"

"Travel? Did you do a lot of competing." he asked intrigued. Morien did a quick double take. - watch yourself she thought.

"Oh, his work was mostly displays. People were always interested in this breed of horse and how it performed. I used to help him."

"Is that how you learnt to vault like that?" Drago asked. "You hardly look strong enough to lift a bale of hay."

"Looks can be deceptive," said Morien steering the conversation away from awkward enquiries. "After all, all that mucking out and grooming one soon develops a muscle or two."

"How many horses did your father have?"

"Five mares and one stallion, Merlin."

"You must have had quite a team of riders." Morien saw the dangerous ground and nodded non-commitally.

"What happened to them when the horses were sold?"

"All went their different ways," lied Morien. "Why don't we swim now?" She changed the subject hastily. They turned the horses back towards the lorry and saw Nina was waving.

"What's up with her?" growled the Baron

"Missing you," murmured Morien suddenly cheeky.

"That's quite enough," he reprimanded under his breath.

Merlin moved into deeper water and soon he was swimming. Drago urged Iatro to follow. So, they headed out to sea. Knowing that it was the Baron's first time, Morien wondered mischievously how he would react when he found he couldn't steer. Did he know that the reins have little impact on a swimming horse and the rider has to depend on legs and weight?

"What an amazing sensation," laughed Drago as he adjusted to the rocking movement. Morien laughed beside him relishing the powerful motion under her. The Baron watched her then and everything inside him turned over. Damn the child, she turned him on simply by being there. He was glad of the water sweeping over him to cool his ardour.

"I think we should go back now. Iatro is tiring."

"OK" she called and swung Merlin around. It was then that Drago realised. He was not in full control.

"Morien," he'd never called her that before. Her heart thumped. "Morien, he won't turn." She laughed ecstatically, the passion of the moment enhancing her apparent wickedness.

"Where's my great horse master now?" she whispered. Drago had to concentrate all his attention on Iatro realising that this was a skill job. Slowly the great horse turned.

"You little witch. Just wait until I get my hands on you. You knew this would happen," he thought. Merlin was swimming back towards him with Morien smiling in triumph. He couldn't take his eyes off this ondine. Her wet T-shirt clung to her, revealing her pointed nipples. Her teeth were glistening as her joy overflowed. Damn her, damn her, damn her. Iatro swung away from the shore again as Merlin approached. Morien leaned down to grab his rein. Just as she had hold of it, she felt the horse find the stability of the sand and Drago inadvertently jerked Iatro away. Morien tumbled into the water. Spluttering and still laughing she surfaced. As Drago had also been holding onto the rein, he was yanked off by her added weight as she fell, landing on top of her.

He wrapped his arms around her and held her hard against him. She had no defence as she was holding onto the reins of both horses. He kissed her salty neck, and his hands began to explore her vibrant body.

"Do you know how much I want to make love to you?" he growled into the lobe of her ear. Morien tensed suddenly becoming aware of her abandoned behaviour. Never before had she reacted in this way. What on earth was the matter with her? His hands wandered over her gently massaging her peaked nipples till she gasped. He pulled her closer.

Suddenly, since she was still holding the reins, a movement of the horses snatched them apart as they walked towards the sand.

Morien felt as though she had been ripped open, her green eyes wide on Drago's face.

What in heaven's name had possessed her? This terrible man held her whole life in the palm of his hand both literally and metaphorically. He thought her a hussy, a toy, a plaything, someone to relieve his arousal. What was more she was behaving like one. She was like a dog on heat. She'd seen enough of that in her time. Now she was so ashamed. This was too much. But she felt she had to play his game to a certain extent to hold her job. She was totally dependent until she qualified. She had to keep her secret for the sake of the Earl. He must never know the truth. She had to keep up the pretence but how long would she be able to resist him? Forcing her feet back on the ground she dragged Merlin onto the beach.

"Saved again," he muttered and turned Iatro's head towards the shore. They swam alongside the horses into the shallows. Without a word, they both vaulted on, and Morien put Merlin into a canter away, away from Drago. He followed at a more sedate walk on the injured Iatro watching his mermaid distancing herself from him. How was he going to handle this? She was an absolute siren and was beginning to become an obsession with him. He realised that he took out his frustration by being angry with her, far angrier than her behaviour merited. He had to keep reminding himself that she was his father's little slut and although, because of that she should be free for the taking, somehow it just didn't feel right. Damn her and damn the old man.

Nina was beside herself with fury when Morien reached the horsebox. "Just what do you think you were doing dragging the Baron into the water like that."

"Oh, did you have your binoculars out?" asked Morien sarcastically.

"It must be extremely dangerous swimming with the horses beside you. The Baron could very easily have been kicked. What are you trying to do to him?"

"We both fell off," was all she said. Her face was wan, her emotions in turmoil. She took a sweat scraper to Merlin to remove the excess water and turned in time to see Iatro up the beach giving himself a violent shake with the Baron clinging on for dear life. By the time he reached them, Merlin was loaded, and Morien was back in her clothes drying her hair.

Nina was all solicitous handing him a towel while he pushed the horse unceremoniously at her. He came over and stood in his all but naked glory staring at Morien. Then abruptly disappeared into the groom's compartment to change. Morien had stared him out then wondered at her audacity. Was this really love, such intense pain that she'd felt as they were pulled apart? The atmosphere on their return was tense and electrified. Nina was gabbling as usual forcing herself between them while Morien tried to become invisible. It was torture back at the yard unloading and settling the horses. Nina got in everyone's way doing virtually nothing. With smouldering eyes, the Baron watched Morien's every move until she escaped into the house for a shower.

CHAPTER 14

There was a definite improvement to Iatro's injury, so the Baron ordered daily trips to the sea. Despite her hopes, he himself did not come again so Morien was detailed to ride Iatro. All the other girls vied for the job of nursemaid and Morien suddenly found herself extremely "popular".

Also, to her great relief Helen withdrew the threat to Merlin, since Morien was back in favour. The swimming treatment slowly improved Iatro's muscles and the fetlock began to heal very quickly. As they returned along the beach one morning Morien decided to experiment with some simple schooling to check for lameness. The horse remained sound so the following day she tried again, forgetting that Gill was riding behind her. Bareback, she was in her element. The horse responded like a dream. Gill was flabbergasted as the big chestnut gathered himself and floated sideways across the sand. Morien noticed her friend's amazement and felt panicky. "You're not to tell. Promise."

"Promise," said Gill speculatively. "I didn't realise you'd got that far with your training," she said ruefully.

"I haven't," lied Morien "I've just been reading something that I wanted to try out and Iatro is so well schooled." Gill said nothing - who did she think she was fooling?

"I suppose now that he's sound, he won't need swimming anymore." sighed Morien "I'd better tell Helen when we get back."

Although the daily swimming of Iatro had been tiring and time consuming, especially since she was now back on lessons, Morien never missed her sessions with Merlin. Nathan now came frequently in the early morning and Drago began to comment on his change of routine.

"Nice to see you for breakfast these days," commented the Baron

"I'd forgotten what I was missing," agreed Nathan sardonically

"Has horse riding become an obsession?"

"I need to go early for like you I have other duties during the day and so does Rankin. It's a bit tiresome having always to depend on someone else. " Nathan excused himself.

"I'm sure you didn't go out so often in the Land Rover, " sneered the Baron.

"Oh, that was not so much fun," rejoined the Earl

"Agreed," acknowledged the Baron non-committaly and left for his early morning session.

As he went to check the mare and foal, he noticed Merlin's empty box and one of the grooms tacking up the ponies for the Earl. Suddenly, it clicked. No wonder he'd felt that things had quietened on that front. He decided to give Nathan a head start and then follow from a distance. Fancy involving Rankin in his clandestine affairs. "Too close by far that one. I suppose he holds the horses while they get together. Pah!!" He felt revolted. He quickly saddled up the horse he was training that morning and came out of the box in time to see his father riding away.

Morien was struggling with Merlin's flying changes when Nathan and Rankin arrived. Merlin was being particularly naughty and welcomed the ponies noisily. She let him rub noses whilst she greeted the others.

"Carry on and let me watch for a while," said Nathan relaxing himself comfortably in the saddle whilst Rankin dismounted allowing the ponies to graze. Morien settled the horse and encouraged him into a regular and contained rhythm. They tried again with a marginally better result.

"It's the weight shift on the second stride that's crucial," called Morien "Then he has time to change on the next stride".

"I'll call it out for you," said Nathan while Morien circled away. As she approached, Nathan called the beat and at last, Merlin caught on. With endless patience and perseverance, the pace became consistent.

"Great," laughed Morien patting Merlin as she came to a stop and allowed him to relax.

"When you've both got your breath back go off and show me a detailed routine using all his paces that he's used to, including lateral movements. Then finish with the one-time changes and see if he's learnt." Nathan and Rankin settled back to enjoy themselves as Morien and Merlin danced together. The sunlight filtered through both mane and hair as they circled against the early morning light. They executed the most complicated manoeuvres with an air of joy about them and finally, in a straight line towards the Earl, they performed a perfect skipping canter.

"Success, success, my dear," cried Nathan clapping his hands. To their horror this was accompanied by a slow handclap as the Baron rode slowly out of the trees.

"So, this is what you do in the dawn," he looked accusingly at all three. Morien quailed and Nathan looked like a naughty boy.

"Hah. So, you've found us at last," he laughed.

"How long has this been going on?" demanded Drago.

"Since I learned to ride," confirmed the Earl

"And you've known about the ability of this horse in my yard and said nothing," accused the Baron.

"I had the feeling you wouldn't have been interested," replied Nathan with irony.

"And this child you've been leading astray, did you teach her?"

"Good heavens no, she and the horse are well ahead of my talents. I'm just the ground jockey."

Morien loathed the way they all constantly talked over her head as though she were a child. Huffily she said that it was late, and she had work to do.

"AND, where is your hat?" came the parting shot from the Baron as she cantered away.

"Oh, Drago, why such a dragon? She's just a harmless child with an immense amount of talent."

"Harmless!! On horseback maybe but look at what she's done to my best horse when I was all set to win this year."

"There seems a certain inconsistency," agreed the Earl. "Helen mentioned that the trouble always occurred when Morien was off duty or on a lesson. Makes you think, doesn't it?" The Baron was dismissive.

"Always her champion! Her trouble is that she's work shy. If you don't mind, I think I'll get back and have a sit on that horse before she feeds it. It may be the answer to my competition hopes. To think you never told me," he said angrily as he left them. Nathan smiled. Maybe things were taking a turn for the better. He was sad Morien was having such a tough time. Perhaps with a mutual interest they could become friends and then he could let the cat out of the bag about the circus.

Back at the yard, the Baron handed his horse to the nearest groom and strode down to Merlin's box.

"Have you fed him yet?" he asked dictatorially

"No," said Morien, astounded.

"Find me a saddle. I'd like to ride him for a few minutes in the school." Morien looked at him mulishly. He stared back until she dropped her eyes. She didn't move.

"I don't often have such a chance."

"He's already worked," was her stubborn response.

He moved towards her, and she backed off. "Please, " he said suddenly. "He obviously has a lot of talent." She turned her back on him. "Please." he whispered close to her ear. She stamped out of the box, speechless with rage as she went to fetch a saddle. Why was she in no position to refuse? No one but she had ridden Merlin since the accident to her father and now this man, this man had the audacity Maybe Merlin would remember the past. I hope he sets him down, she thought maliciously as she returned with Merlin's saddle.

In her absence, the Baron had made friends. Oh, the fickleness, thought Morien as she saddled the horse and led him out. News had got around the yard and the girls were all agog. Morien was aware of a pied piper trail behind them. Together they entered the school and the Baron mounted. Sadly, Merlin had already been worked so he acquiesced to the strange rider. He was supple from his earlier exercise and ready to come to hand immediately. Some of his responses were slow as he tried to interpret the slight differences in the commands, but he looked magnificent.

Morien was now even more aware of the other girls. They were looking from her to the horse and whispering together. Her ostracism was complete. She would never be one of them again since her superior riding knowledge was being demonstrated for them all.

She brushed away a tear. How her father, the man she had loved so dearly, would have enjoyed Merlin's progress. Instead it was the hateful Baron who was reaping all the pleasure. No matter what he asked, Merlin gave it one hundredfold. He floated, lengthened, shortened, danced through every complicated movement in the book and Drago looked as though he grew from the horse's back, so close in harmony were they.

After ten minutes, the Baron dismounted and gave the horse a good pat plus a piece of carrot from his pocket. Handing the horse to Morien "Thank you " he said. "tell me about his background . oh, and yours as well for that matter." he demanded.

Morien looked away. She still had her promise to the Earl. How was she going to deal with this? "There's nothing to tell," she hedged as they walked back to the yard, then winced at his expostulation.

"Why the mystery?"

"There's no mystery. He was trained by my father."

"Quite an accomplished rider "

"Yes," she was non-committal

He tried persuasion. "Tell me about your father."

"He died recently." Morien's eyes filled and Drago realising he had touched the fragile nerve once more, although he was not too sure that it was not part of her act. She roughly pulled on Merlin's bridle, trying to outpace him.

"Well, all right, we'll leave it for now." Drago changed his tack. "Since it was your fault that I have no horse for the Championships, I think it would be politic for you to offer me yours." he looked straight into her wide green eyes, bright with unshed tears. He could see that battle going on in them. When she didn't answer, he tried another angle.

"We could have a truce."

"Do I have any choice?" she asked ignoring the remark.

"Well," reluctantly "yes, I suppose so."

"What's that supposed to mean?"

"That I cannot order you but, I am not prepared to crawl to you." Morien chose to ignore the implication of that remark as they reached the stable and untacked the horse.

"What will it entail?" she wanted to know at last. The Baron let out a deep sigh and she realised that he had been holding his breath.

"Well, he's not qualified for the major event, but he can be entered in a couple of local shows to try for some points. There's a chance he could make it if he behaves in public." A sparkle came back into Morien's eyes as he added "I'd also like to enter him in the Kür - that is freestyle dressage to music. That is the big event that Iatro was being prepared for. It's an opportunity for both horse and rider to express themselves creatively without the restriction of a previously laid-down series of movements."

83

It was all so close to what Merlin had originally been trained for that Morien could not resist. What, after all, had she to lose? Still why couldn't it have been her father in the saddle. She looked askance at him, knowing how much this request must matter to him. Could she make him beg? Wickedly she extended her moment of power, since she could feel the Baron's suspense. After all he had put her through, let him sweat a little. There was another advantage too, she realised, that if any further catastrophes occurred, he was unlikely to throw her out during the next few weeks. She would be safe until after the competition. Still he shouldn't have it all his own way. She looked at him for what felt like minutes, his slim elegance, in the close-fitting breeches, his broad well-muscled shoulders, the smouldering eyes watching her under the brim of his hat, the epitome of masculinity. She shuddered slightly at the implication of those eyes as the fire inside her began to flame up. How she longed for him to hold her close in his arms.

"All right," she said. He grasped her hand "As long as I stay involved in his training." Drago hesitated and almost withdrew his hand. Then clasping it tighter "OK, it's a deal .and a truce?"

She nodded. He drew her against him, but she held herself stiff and unresiliant, turning her head so that his lips only brushed her hair. "I wonder why you pretend to know nothing. What is your game? You certainly are a very good actress. One day, you will tell me all," he said smiling as he released her. His smile threw her completely off balance. She was devastated when he switched on the charm. As he walked happily away, she was filled with misgivings, especially when she saw Nina lying in wait for him.

"I was surprised to see you on that horse, she commented loudly so that Morien could hear her. "Not really your level or quality".

"On the contrary, my dear. He's a bit of secret magic. He's incredibly supple and light." Nina looked put out. "That girl's father must have been quite a master."

"He obviously didn't teach her anything." Nina sneered "Just look what she's managed to do to the horses around here. Funny how hers is all right." She watched as Morien headed for the tack room away from such a malicious tongue. The Baron made a non-committal grunt.

"Do you think she has manipulated the whole situation?" she asked pensively.

"What do you mean?"

"Well, it's one way of getting your attention, albeit somewhat deceitfully. Puts your horse out of action and then, miracle of miracles, here's a suitable replacement." The Baron stopped and looked full at Nina. He didn't say a word, simply looked. Nina backed away with a nervous laugh. "Just a thought," she murmured, as he turned on his heel and left her.

CHAPTER 15

Gill caught up with Morien. "Hey. What's up with the Baron riding Merlin?"

"I got found out," confessed Morien

"What do you mean 'found out'?"

"Well, I've been schooling Merlin up in the woods on the days when we don't go for a stretch. He loves to dance and play so I was working on flying changes."

"Gosh, that's pretty advanced for a five-year-old," said Gill surprised.

"Is it?" queried Morien "Dad's other horses were the same."

Gill looked non-plussed

"Anyway, sometimes the Earl and Rankin stopped to watch now that the Earl uses a pony to get about."

"Wow, the Earl? I should have been terribly nervous."

"Oh no you wouldn't. He's such a kind person and so interested. Today we arranged that he would help me with the changes which were going wrong. You know it's easier to see why from the ground."

"That explains how you were able to get Iatro going on the beach. You're an expert."

"Oh no, I'm not."

"Mm." acknowledged Gill

"Well, there we were putting the whole thing together when the Baron arrived. I've never been so embarrassed in my life. He'd obviously been watching from the trees."

"How awful. I wondered why he was riding out. He never does. He always uses the school."

"Search me," said Morien "He must have followed the Earl."

"So, what's the situation now?" Gill wanted to know.

"Well, it seems he thinks I deliberately injured Iatro through carelessness, so he wants to take Merlin to the next competition as a replacement."

"What?"

"Yes. The trouble is that I don't really have any choice since I can't prove that I wasn't responsible for the neglect of his horses. He wants the ride as a quid pro quo."

"Quite honestly, Morien, if there's a mess you certainly know how to fall in it."

As they returned to the yard the whole place was buzzing with the news that the Baron had been riding Merlin and that the horse had lots of hidden talents. Morien beat a hasty retreat to avoid having to answer awkward questions. All the girls crowded around Gill who showed off a bit because she had seen Morien get a tune out of Iatro on the beach. Morien had begged her not to tell she explained, but now the secret was out Gill swanked with the news. Nina, however, was quite malicious.

"I don't know what Drago is thinking about. The horse isn't even shod. He seems besotted with anything on four legs that can prance, and that child is so incompetent," she sniffed.

"I'd like to see you produce those paces on a horse," retorted Gill defensively.

"I don't need to to jump," she responded sarcastically

"That's what you think," muttered Gill under her breath.

That evening after supper, Morien received a summons to the Hall from the Baron. What on earth did he want now, she wondered, quickly showering and looking for something respectable to wear. It simply wasn't fair. The one thing that had made life here bearable had been her daily rides on her own horse. Apart from her work, he was her life. And now that monster was going to get all the pleasure. She couldn't work the horse twice in a day. What would he do to Merlin, introducing all his subtly different instructions? Would the horse end up confused? She began to panic. "I am such an idiot," she thought. "It's about time I stood up to him instead of letting him ride rough-shod over me. After all who does he think he is?"

Pushing her hair back behind her ears she glared at her reflection - that's right more aggression! Then she burst out laughing. No point in getting into an entirely negative mood. Perhaps all this could be to her advantage.

She made her way down to the Hall where she found Nathan ensconced in his favourite chair. As she entered the room, he could not help but notice her natural grace and elegance. Anyone would be forgiven thinking of her as aristocracy. Pity his son didn't think so.

"Come in, come in, my dear," he greeted her. "I hear you've been summoned." his eyes twinkled.

"Yes. We certainly both fell in it this morning, didn't we?" said Morien returning his smile. "Did he have a real go at you?"

"Nothing I couldn't handle."

"I'm so relieved. He certainly seems to have entirely the wrong impression about you and me."

"What do you mean?"

Morien flushed "Well, you know …."

"No, I don't, my dear."

"Well, you remember my first evening when he caught me giving you a thank you hug?"

"Yes," he said guardedly

"He seems to think I am your paramour." Nathan looked shocked.

"Oh, I thought that just the heat of the moment, a passing observation," he mused

"Oh no. He's constantly reminding me of it." Nathan hid a smile as he pictured his son jealous of him – well, well.

"What does he say?"

"Well, it's mainly insinuation, that I'm a flirt and am after every man I see, especially you."

"Don't let it bother you."

"I try not to but I've never been one for the boys, never really had time for a boyfriend even."

"I can see that it's upsetting. I'll have a word with him."

"Oh no, don't do that. It will only deepen his convictions if he thinks I've been telling tales."

"Mm, I see – quite a quandary."

"Don't worry about me. I'll survive. I just realise how lucky I am to be getting this training with a roof over my head." Morien sat herself down.

"It seems my son was impressed by his little ride earlier." commented the Earl

"Yes," said Morien reluctantly. "He certainly asked for every pace in the book and Merlin played completely into his hands."

"You are not pleased?"

"Yes and no," she responded "No one has ridden Merlin but my father and me. I am having difficulty in accepting the situation."

"That is hard, I'll agree. But as long as he's riding your horse you can feel more secure here when things go wrong."

"I suppose it has its merits," she responded.

"I understand you are being blamed for Iatro's injury. That does put you in rather an invidious position. "

"You can say that again."

"We really must find a way to disabuse him of his misconceptions."

"And fly to the moon," murmured Morien

"I regret that, for your sake, but I do find it rather amusing that he'll inadvertently find out something he never wanted to know. Not that that helps you, my dear."

"Oh?" enquired Morien

"He's never, but never sat on a horse of Merlin's standard that's been anything but classically trained."

"Yes, it's ironic isn't it. At least it will be a completely unbiased assessment," said Nathan.

"What I find difficult," mused Morien "is what I would call over analysis – one leg here, the other one there. From watching the other pupils, I see all sorts of contradictions."

"How's that?"

"Well, I learned that if you stiffen the horse stops naturally, but I see riders who are so stiff and tense from concentrating and nerves. With their minds, they want the horse to go forward but their bodies are telling it to stop."

"Interesting point. Have you discussed this with Drago?"

"I wouldn't dare," she laughed.

Nathan winked as Drago appeared and greeted Morien on his best behaviour.

"We have to choose some music for Merlin to work to. Because we are so short of time and you are familiar with his movement, I need you to listen to one or two pieces." Morien was intrigued.

"The music centre is in the study. Come," summoned the Baron.

Morien glanced uncertainly at Nathan, but he gestured that she should follow. They went through into a large, airy room with a business-like desk in one corner with a number of filing cabinets, antiqued to match the room. A sofa and several comfortable chairs were arranged to benefit from the light and the positioning of the hi fi speakers. Down one side the walls were lined with books, cassettes, CDs and video tapes. Morien was conscious of being alone with Drago where no one would interrupt. Why the room was almost soundproof.

"First of all, I would like to show you a video of a performance by the Spanish Riding School in Vienna where I trained." She leaned cautiously against the sofa watching him checking the video.

"Aren't you going to sit? I don't bite you know," he said measuringly, his eyes wandering over her full length. Nervously she perched on the arm, not noticing his sardonic expression. The beauty of the movement of the white horses transfixed her as they gracefully danced to the music of Mozart.

As she watched, the horses reminded her of her lost troupe, the horses she's had lost to survive. They were just like the horses in the film, same colour, same conformation, same joyous movement, even the airs above the ground. She felt as though she was watching her father. The only difference was the riders, all dressed in military uniforms on tooled leather saddles instead of bareback. She felt tears coming and a physical wrench as she wondered how her beloved animals were faring now.

She could see, at last, why the Baron was so prejudiced about circuses. It was a bit like comparing ballet dancing with musical comedy, although her father's routines had included some of these complicated manoeuvres.

"The riders look so smart and solemn. The horses are so beautiful and all matching." Morien was transfixed.

"Yes, as you know all the horses there are Lippizaners coming mostly from the Lipica Stud in Slovenia."

"I had no idea there were such beautiful displays," thrilled Morien.

"You mean you've never heard of the Spanish Riding School?"

"No, not at all. Just fancy having an indoor riding school with crystal chandeliers."

"This simply doesn't make sense," he muttered "With your obvious knowledge you're simply prevaricating again." Morien turned puzzled eyes on him. Why should he think she was pretending to be surprised and captivated? She actually was.

"You cannot possibly train your horse at that standard and be so ignorant of others. Anyone would think you'd been living in a cloister."

Yes, thought Morien, that just about summed up the circus life – a totally enclosed community.

The film ended. "Come." Drago took her arm and guided her over to the table where he'd laid out some charts that he had drawn up. He explained how they created the patterns to obtain a flowing sequence.

"This is what I was working on with Iatro," touching her hand as he shifted the sheets. He showed her a series of designs in rectangles which represented the different movements and paces. Morien wanted him to hold her hand forever but pulled it away ostensibly to point to something. He smiled.

"I'll play the music I was using so you can follow the sequences." Soft lyrical sounds filled the room as he switched on the cassette. When he returned to the table, he gently twisted a strand of her hair. Fire again shot through her and instinctively she drew away taunted by his flirting. He pretended not to notice, and her eyes were drawn to his elegant and powerful fingers tracing the patterns with the music. Morien found concentration difficult being more and more conscious of his overpowering masculinity.

"You see here," he was saying enthusiastically as she surreptitiously glanced at his long eyelashes, "Because Iatro was stiff to the left, we could really contain his energy through this loop and burst out across the arena."

He's too beautiful, she thought knowing her responses spelt danger and trouble.

"Are you listening?"

"Oh yes, yes. I'm beginning to get the picture."

"Have you any music in mind that would suit Merlin?" he asked hopefully. "I've got a really good selection." The razzmatazz of circus music filled her mind and momentarily transported, she closed her eyes seeing the gaiety and smelling the sawdust. Images flowed of the liberty horses entering the arena at a smart canter to the cheers of the crowds. After several brisk circuits, they used to slow into graceful turns and loops allowing the riders to somersault and scissor over and under, floating sideways, drifting back until the music speeded up again for the finale. It was a mixture of noisy with classical. She tried to recall the name of the entrance music.

`"Do you have " she hummed a few bars

91

"I think so." he responded and went to look thinking it was rather jazzy.

"I think he also likes a bit of Schubert," she laughed.

Gradually over the next hour she relaxed becoming more and more absorbed as they tried different melodies, making notes and sketching patterns. He watched her surreptitiously as her silky hair obscured her face. Suddenly, she tossed it back triumphantly indicating the final layout to the last piece of music.

"I think this will work. Let's try it out tomorrow," she said with delight

The intensity of his gaze arrested her, eyes wide, lips suggestively apart, mesmerised she waited as he leant over her and possessed her lips, his tongue demanding and insinuating. His arms encased her, and she melted helplessly against him as his kiss became more persistent and his hands began to explore her breasts. He pulled her hard against him and she could feel his arousal. Fire shot through her body as her heart beat overtime and she ran out of breath. She wanted him desperately and completely. Madness, madness.

Never had she experienced such ecstatic emotions. She had to stop. Now. But she didn't want to. Suddenly, she struggled free, drawing blood in the process, aghast at her behaviour.

"What on earth do you think you are doing?" She flew into the attack trying to sound really affronted.

"Well, my beauty, not so easily bridled." His scorn was clear to see as he dabbed his cut lip. "I don't see why my father should have exclusivity."

"Why not? " Asked Morien, still trembling. "What else has he got to brighten his life?"

She suddenly saw this misunderstanding as a subterfuge, a haven. "You have a demanding charm, but I prefer older men." She firmly kept her thoughts on her father and old Renaldo and the shuddering calmed down. Gino and Drago were two of a kind. "You have plenty of more willing ladies. Don't be greedy."

"You know you want me almost as much as I want you," was his candid reply. "When I touch you, you burst into flames."

"I don't know what you mean," blushingly hiding her face.

"Coyness doesn't become you," was his retort. Once more in deep water, Morien tossed her head in apparent defiance. She must brazen it out like the hussy he thought her, as becoming business-like again, he said: "We'll work with Merlin first thing in the morning. Have him in the school at six."

Morien looked at her watch. "10.30 p.m. already."

"Go and get your beauty sleep." He ached to touch her again but resisted as he escorted her to the door. "I'd better see you off the premises in case you try to sneak back to my father. From now on I want the best out of you." he said suggestively.

Morien stuck her nose in the air and didn't deign to reply as she retreated to her part of the house. Sleep came slowly as all the excitement of the evening and the plans for Merlin raced around her head. She knew she must develop a stratcgy to handlc Drago and keep him at arm's length, keep playing the older man theme. She needed to inform Nathan in case he acted on their earlier conversation and chastised his son. It was going to be difficult to explain her change of mind without admitting to the rash behaviour and her true feelings. Arm's length, which seemed to be the only language he understands. She fell into a dreamless sleep.

CHAPTER 16

At last Morien felt she could relax. Things were going well and whilst the Baron worked with Merlin now each morning, she was allowed to bring Iatro back into training. Merlin took to the competition schooling like a duck to water and it was decided that he should be entered at the next affiliated competition for the Novice and Elementary classes. The Baron wanted to assess his performance in the public arena with all its distractions.

"He's going so well now that I'm going to enter him at Lingfield next weekend. He needs some competition experience and points."

"Tell me about the points," asked Morien

"To reach the top of recognised competition each horse has to be registered with the British Horse Society. It is then entered into affiliated competitions where points can be won by coming in the top echelons. As you accumulate points so you can qualify for regional, national and international competitions. It keeps a good standard."

"You think Merlin can win some so soon?"

"He's got to and quickly if I'm to ride him in the Kür."

Morien had a moment of unease over the registration with the British Horse Society in order to gain points.

"I've got the registration forms here. Let's complete them and mail them today." Drago asked for details of Merlin's age, exact colour and breeding. Morien was suitably vague.

"C'mon, you must know something about him. Where did your father buy him?"

"No idea. He just went off occasionally and came back with another grey horse."

"Oh well, that'll have to do for now. Let's get this in the post."

"I'd like Helen to ride Merlin in this first class. She had the considerable competition experience that you lack. I don't want to arouse too much interest on Merlin's first outing. Helen's a good jockey. She knows the tests through and through." For some reason the Baron did not want to attract too much attention to the horse by riding it himself. Morien was dumbstruck.

"But he's mine," she burst out.

"Are you in favour of the blind leading the blind leaving him with bad memories or do you want him to succeed?" What could she say? There was no other answer than "Let her ride, but I want to be there and to be totally involved." Drago laughed at her earnest determined face.

"Agreed. Incidentally get some copies of the tests and start learning them. Don't teach them to Merlin though or he'll anticipate the sequence of movements and spoil things."

Morien was so excited when show day came. Merlin was in a high mood as he was loaded with Crystabelle and two other horses belonging to clients. Morien was utterly dismayed when, as always, Nina got herself chosen to groom for the day, Helen being under the misapprehension that that was what the Baron wanted. Morien was beside herself as Nina did everything in her power to push her into the background until even Helen became exasperated.

Drago sensing the conflict, asked Nina to confine her work to Crystabelle and Dolphin, leaving Noddy and Merlin to Morien. Nina was pleased as she would be dealing exclusively with the Baron. Since only Helen and Drago were riding, Helen asked Morien to work in Merlin for her and get him used to the showground.

The whole procedure was a complete mystery to Morien. All around the large park land there appeared to be delineated areas with letters around them, which she suddenly realised were a replica of the indoor school at the stables. Helen, riding Noddy, joined her briefly and explained the procedure.

"You've seen the test sheets. The judge sits in her car at one end and gives marks for each designated set of movements. Each rider is given a pre-arranged time to present themselves.   I'm due in Arena 5 in 10 minutes with Noddy. Then I'll need Merlin immediately as there are only 15 minutes before the next test. I hope the arenas are running to time as it's pretty close."

Morien followed Helen to the warm-up area where quite a number of other horses were working. With Merlin, she concentrated of circles at a good rhythmic trot. They were in their element and Morien noticed they were beginning to attract a lot of attention. For a while she stayed and secretly showed off but then, remembering the Baron's caution, she took off for a walk around the showground to get him used to the sights and sounds, leaving Helen working with Noddy.

When she got back to the lorry park, she found Nina was fawning over the Baron much to Morien's amusement. She could sense his irritation, though carefully controlled.

"Ride Crystabelle round and cool her down before boxing her," he commanded. Nina couldn't wait to comply and coyly waited for a leg-up. He helped her into the saddle and then slapped the horse encouragingly on the rump. It was some moments before Nina's glee evaporated on realising that she'd been dismissed, and she rode sulkily away. Morien couldn't help grinning to herself as she prepared Merlin for Helen. Drago led Dolphin off the lorry and attached a lunge line.

"Enough smirking, madam," he murmured. "You can lunge Dolphin while I watch Merlin's test."

Morien could hardly contain her disappointment. Merlin's first public showing, and she couldn't watch. "Now, don't you start sulking too," said the Baron testily. "You can watch the second one. It's much more interesting than the Novice. I need to be there to give Helen back-up if she needs it." Understanding the logic, but still resentful, Morien led Dolphin to an empty space and began working her on the lunge.

Watching surreptitiously, she saw Helen mount up and was delighted when she came to work nearby. Merlin didn't go nearly so well for her as he did for Morien and Drago, but he still attracted attention and several people followed down to the arena to watch his test. Morien tried to concentrate on Dolphin who was slowly loosening up. She noticed Nina on Crystabelle move over to get a better view of Helen and Drago. She seemed ever so subtly to have obscured Morien's view. Surprise, surprise. After ten minutes Morien took Dolphin back to the lorry and, since there was no sign of Nina, she prepared the horse for the Baron to ride. Suddenly, Nina trotted up.

"You should have seen him. He was thoroughly disobedient, refusing to enter the arena and then spooking at everything in sight." Morien was horrified. He'd never done that before. Helen and Baron came back leading Merlin with Helen looking thoroughly disconsolate. "I really let you down, Morien, " she said. "He just wouldn't listen to me."

"It is my fault," said the Baron. "I should have ridden him myself. He is not familiar with you and all the new sights and sounds set him off. He really is above himself."

96

Morien wanted to protest at such criticism. "It's all a matter of absorbing and using the gaiety, "she said.

"You don't need to tell Drago what to do," simpered Nina. "It's in the training and this one is obviously lacking."

Drago looked at her sharply since she had inadvertently insulted him as well through association and then commented with false mildness. "Please get Crystabelle and Noddy ready for travelling. Helen, you take Dolphin. It's Elementary 24 in Arena 7 and you've got ten minutes. He's used to you so you shouldn't have any trouble. I'll take Merlin."

With that he swung into the saddle and rode off on Merlin. Tentatively Morien followed. Let Nina look after both horses for once. She watched intrigued as the Baron carefully developed a rapport with the horse. His body and Merlin's became united in one perfect movement, fluid and fascinating. Slowly the horse came to hand.

"Seems Drago's got a new horse," said a voice behind her. "Stylish looking beast," was the response. "Yes, looks pretty powerful. Got some nice paces." "That's an understatement," rejoined the other. "Well, he could get a tune out of a camel." laughed the woman. After further ribaldry, they moved away.

Drago rode over to her. "We're in arena 5. Follow us down." Merlin nuzzled Morien who whispered to him.

"Going to wish me luck?" he asked quizzically

"Yes, good luck," she nodded. "I've told him to behave himself."

Of course, it was inevitable that Merlin should perform perfectly for the Baron. Morien watched delightedly as the horse showed his paces absolutely accurately. From initial entrance to final bow, he never put a foot wrong. Thus, he won his first red rosette. She could tell that even for the Baron, it was an accolade being Merlin's first competition.

The Baron was well pleased since it proved he had a chance at the major competition in a few weeks.

On the way home, Nina and Morien were forced into each other's company in the grooms' compartment of the horsebox. There was no disguising Nina's jealousy.

"It's about time you realised," she said sarcastically, "that people like you should keep their station."

"I don't know what you mean," responded Morien

"Pushing yourself and your horse forward all the time. There are other animals you know."

"I don't remember being given much choice," said Morien with spirit

"Well, what's his background?"

"That's my business."

"You see what I mean. No breeding and secretive as well."

"What's that to do with anything? I'm only here to work and get qualified."

"That's rich," sneered Nina. "The only work you concentrate on is chasing the Baron and look what's happened to his horses in your care." In the restricted space, Morien turned her back on Nina.

"What nothing to say?" taunted Nina. She'd obviously struck a nerve. Still Morien refused to be drawn. She could feel Nina's anger now.

"Well let me tell you, the Baron enjoys a bit of superficial flirting, but his heart belongs to his horses, so cool off."

"I think you insult him," said Morien "and since when did you become his keeper?"

"We've had an arrangement for over a year now and he's on the point of proposing. He just wants to get this special competition over." Morien felt cold and hurt inside which was exactly what Nina was looking for. Then she rallied. Who needs him anyway?

"I don't like your wicked insinuations," Morien stated firmly, suddenly fed up with being sat upon. "I hope he doesn't regret his decision if he makes one. You would do well to remember that horses, as you said, are his first love," she said smugly.

"Now you are being insulting," said Nina

"Oh, I couldn't possible compete with you," replied Morien, flashing her a sweet smile. Fortunately, they had arrived back at the yard and Morien jumped out as the vehicle came to a stop. Amid the ensuing bustle, she had no further contact with Nina. But a perfect day was spoiled.

CHAPTER 17

At last, the horses were settled, fed and watered and Morien was in Merlin's box watching him contentedly munching. She had recovered from her contretemps with Nina.

"Well, young fellow, how did you enjoy your outing? Bit different from the last time." As she hugged him, she was aware of a shadow at the door. The Baron appeared.

"All settled?" he asked. Morien nodded.

"He went very well today. I couldn't be happier with his performance. I hope you are pleased too." She nodded.

"I'd like you to have this since it is his first." He smiled his dazzling smile and gave her the red rosette. She didn't understand him - so autocratic and yet so understanding at the same time. Then he caught her off guard.

"When was the last time, the last outing?" he queried. Morien hesitated, which was not lost on the Baron, then thought quickly.

"Oh, on the journey over here when we first arrived," she said brightly. "Then we didn't know what the future would hold for us."

"Fabricating again, "sighed the Baron.

"Yes", she smiled mischievously.

"Oh well, no doubt one day you'll tell me." As she came out the stable door Morien was aware of the intensity of his gaze. He placed his hand over hers as she drew the bolt and helped her fasten it. Then she felt rather than saw the change in Drago as she caught sight of Nina walking towards them. After the brief moment of intimacy, he had donned once more his professional cloak.

"Drago, darling, Jenny has invited us over to her place for a celebratory drink. Would 8.00 p.m. be OK?" There was an imperceptible sigh.

"I don't feel in the mood at the moment." Nina pouted and linked her arm in his. The pride and the poison thought Morien unkindly. Then she heard him say:

"I have things to sort out with Morien regarding the Kür, whilst Merlin's performance is still clear in my mind, so not tonight." Morien beat a hasty retreat. Any more of Nina's venom and she'd throw up. The Baron caught up with her with Nina

99

trailing. "Please come to the house immediately after your dinner."

"I'm tired," Morien said blushing, recalling the last time.

"I know," he responded.

"I'll not be your pawn to bait Nina." His eyes hurt.

"I'm sorry," he said "That was not my intention. Sleep well." Nina watched them go their separate ways.

Morien's feelings were completely haywire. Once more her tongue had got the better of her. Two enemies in one day were quite an achievement. Why were people so difficult to live with? Give me animals any day. Was she supposed to go to the house or not? She felt sure it was only an excuse. No doubt she'd get a summons if he really wanted her. Really wanted her, just the thought produced a response in her. No - shut him out. She'd have an early night.

The next morning, she struggled sleepily down to breakfast and was just relaxing with a cup of tea when Gill appeared looking agitated.

"Morien, come quickly. Merlin's loose," she cried

Tiredness and tea forgotten Morien leapt to her feet and ran after the departing Gill. Visions of broken legs, horrid cuts raced through her mind. She reached the yard to find it in uproar. She soon saw the reason why. There, grazing happily in the paddock with the Baron's special mare was Merlin. There was no doubting his relationship with the mare as she nuzzled him gently. He must have jumped the fence.

Morien was thunderstruck as the implications flooded over her: the special mare; her inability to conceive; this possibly being her last chance for this season. "Am I some sort of Jonah?" she thought in panic. Several of the girls who were gossiping at the fence fell silent as Morien approached.

"Here, you'd better have this," said Gill handing her a head collar. "We tried to catch him for you, but he won't let any of us anywhere near him." Taking the head collar, she knew without turning that the Baron was coming as a sudden silence fell. Quickly she vaulted over the fence and called to Merlin. Being a stallion never since he was a foal had he run free, and he was enjoying it. He tossed his head and moved protectively to the mare as Morien approached. He made a little rush at her and,

100

when she didn't back off like the other girls, he started pawing and snorting.

"Do be careful," called Gill

The mare was nervous of Morien. Suddenly she took off and Merlin, with a prance, followed. They dropped into a long striding floating trot, as they crossed the paddock and came to a halt, tails held high. In the early morning sunlight, they looked ethereal. They were so happy Morien hardly wanted to spoil it all. She stood her ground and called Merlin again. He whickered. She held her breath and then, very reluctantly, he walked over to her. The mare followed. She slipped the head collar over his head, and he pulled her gently to the mare nuzzling her to stroke her.

Then very sadly and dejectedly, she led him out of the field. The mare and foal protested at his departure, and he pranced a little showing off at them. Morien looked neither to left or right, taking him firmly into his box. There was no point in chastising him. He had followed his natural instincts and secretly she couldn't help being proud of him and his little "family".

It was obvious that he had been out all night as the box was relatively clean and the hay net almost untouched. She just stood there with her cheek against his neck waiting for the storm to break. She knew the Baron was standing at the door, but she felt completely drained and empty. For such a heinous crime, there was only one punishment. Then she heard him sigh and the sound of his retreating footsteps.

She was still in shock when Gill eventually came for her, still hanging onto Merlin's mane. She felt her numb fingers being disentangled.

"Helen says the Baron is waiting to exercise Merlin in the new routines. Please hurry. I've brought his tack."

"He can't. I can't." Morien trailed off miserably.

"Now, come on, snap out of it. At least if he wants to ride, you're not getting the boot."

"You're right. I'm being a wimp. It's just that ..oh never mind."

"It's just that ..too many things are happening," commented Gill sagely. "Stop being so vulnerable."

"Please take Merlin down for me. I can't take a confrontation at the moment."

Gill took the reins and led Merlin away. Like an automaton, Morien mucked out and set fair. Why, oh why? Who was it that wanted her gone? Did this person know that she had nowhere to go, that she would be literally on the street? Probably not. Such behaviour smacked of absolute selfishness with little thought for the consequences, but that was Nina all over. She remembered her vituperous conversation with Nina. Drooping she attended to all her other duties around the yard, knowing that when the exercising sessions were over, she would no doubt be summoned. And so, it was. She now stood before him in the office.

"Why do you do this to me?" he asked with ominous quiet. "Can't you even shut a stable door correctly?" Morien turned blank-eyed to look at him.

"You know it was shut. I   you we did it together," she stumbled.

"Yes, yes, I recall. But you went back later, to say good night didn't you, didn't you, instead of coming up to the house as I had asked?" Morien dropped her head.   "You go every evening so why should last night have been different?"   Denial was pointless, how could she prove it was untrue?

"You knew I'd be safely out of the way. I waited up for you, you know."

A blank numbness took hold of Morien. He never gave her a chance. And why should he believe her anyway. She had no defence, no alibi.

"What have you got to say for yourself? The cat got your tongue?"

"I'll make arrangements for us to leave at the end of the week," she said flatly.

"You will not," was the response. "You forget that horse is entered for a competition that I particularly want to win."

"Yes, but after what he's apparently done," gasped Morien.

"We won't know for a week or two whether he's succeeded where others have failed.   With her history, you may be reprieved." Morien breathed again momentarily, then he said, "How do I know that this is the first time?"

"You are forthwith suspended from all horse care. You will attend to your horse's stable, but only when I have the horse out for exercise. Others will shut the door. Your other time will be

102

spent here in the office on administration. Helen has been asking for help for some time and quite frankly I don't know what else to do with you for the next few weeks. Let's hope that you don't cause too much damage in here."

Morien did not know how to react, so she simply walked out. Without thinking she made her way to the Hall to see the Earl. Rankin let her in. Nathan looked at her woebegone face.

"Now what has happened?" he enquired. Morien couldn't hold back the tears at this first sympathetic word and went into his outstretched arms. He let her cry on and on until exhaustion overtook her. Then slowly it all came out.

"I feel as though some spiteful gremlin is haunting me," she said at last, not wishing to cast blame without evidence. "How would I ever let my precious horse escape? He's my whole life. Why would I want to damage the Baron's horses, Iatro and the mare?"

"We don't know why fate deals us these blows, my child. What we do know is that we overcome them as best we can and learn from them. Every time you are knocked over, you must rise stronger than before. As you are aware, I know of these things. Pain is a great teacher."

"I know, I know, but it is so easy to say."

"I think it's time you called Rankin to get me a dry sweater before I catch my death," said Nathan with a grin. Morien had to smile. He was so elfin and practical. Rankin soon dealt with the wet clothing, also bringing Morien a wet flannel for her face. Then he miraculously produced tea and biscuits. As Morien poured the tea Nathan mused.

"You know, such a foal of Merlin and this mare could be quite special. Both he and the mare certainly move well."

"My father always said his horses were very well bred. I never really asked him"

"Maybe Drago won't be quite so displeased."

"Oh, but I can't tell him, can I?"

"No, maybe this isn't a good time because your true history will out and Drago will feel doubly duped." They sat in thought, sipping their tea.

"I had hoped today would be a happy one for you," said Nathan eventually. Morien looked up.

103

"The circus is coming to town in a couple of weeks. I thought on your day off we could sneak off together to see Renaldo." He could hardly believe the transformation his words had wrought.

"You're teasing me," she said breathlessly. Nothing, nothing could be as good as seeing Renaldo.

"No. It's absolutely true. Which is your day off?"

"Tuesday." Her face fell. "That is if I'm allowed out."

"Let's see how the land lies." Although happy for her, Nathan looked a little whimsical at her reaction. He hoped there was a little space in her heart for him as she gave him a departing hug.

CHAPTER 18

As Merlin was back in his box there was no exercising today, so Morien joined Helen in the office, which was a hive of activity when she arrived. Helen had just put down the 'phone when it rang again. Jean was frantically typing and seemed to be surrounded by files and papers.

It was a square brightly lit room that Morien had not been in since her first day. What a lot had happened since then. She recalled her unexpected summons just as Helen was explaining all. What a turning point that day had turned out to be. She recalled the warmth of Nathan and the terror of his son. She had been a crab without its shell, totally vulnerable to the unfamiliarity. Her stomach still tended to turn over at the memory. Helen put down the 'phone.

"I know it sounds selfish of me after all your trauma, but I really appreciate having some help."

"Do you handle all this by yourself?" Morien asked.

"Pretty well. We have Jean on the phones whom you've met already. She's a real Girl Friday, knows nearly as much about the business as me and there's a bookkeeper called Bob. Do you type?"

"No but I'm willing to learn - right now - I used to play a keyboard. It can't be that difficult."

"Good."

Being in the office, she began to understand the complications of running the business, why there was regimentation and how it worked. It made a lot of sense. Apart from all the staff, students and clients who needed organising, there were over forty horses on the yard, each with its individual diet and requirements. Maintaining food stocks could be quite involved. There were the regular visits from the farrier to be planned, including the occasional emergencies. The vet visited periodically for accidents as well as general health.

"Here are the horse lists," said Helen handing Morien some charts. "You will see that there are two - one for client allocation for lessons or student training sessions and the other is the housekeeping one which covers everything - feeding, shoeing, veterinary, saddlery, grooms etc." Morien examined the columns, seeing her name crossed off from Crystabelle and Iatro.

Then there were all the different courses for pupils and clients. There were horses brought in for training, the training of the resident horses not to mention the entire breeding programme. Moreover, she had to remember the machinery and the vehicles. With her circus experience, Morien understood the reasoning for much of the planning and programming since it couldn't have functioned without.

"We have to synchronise everything. Can't have a horse with the farrier when a client needs it."

"What's this bit marked land maintenance?" she asked

"Well, that's really the Earl's province. To keep the land in good condition we have to rotate horses with cattle and sometimes leave the land fallow. Grass is really a crop." It was a whole new area for Morien. She really enjoyed it and decided to ask the Earl about it.

Helen later told the Baron that Morien showed a remarkable aptitude for the business side, and he was amazed when he heard she was teaching herself to type. Not only had she brightened up but was actually enjoying her punishment. It appeared the Baron found her to be an enigma.

Time rushed past. Helen came in with cups of coffee.

"Here," she said. "Take a break now."

"Thanks, could really do with that," said Morien.

"What do you think of office work?"

"It seems such a maze but it's beginning to make sense. I don't have any choice really,"

"Well, you do seem to get on the wrong side of the Baron. Sad really because he's incredibly kind."

"Oh, come on. I've seen absolutely no sign of that," retorted Morien.

"I have personal experience," said Helen. "Some years back, when I was a student, I was on a jumping lesson, riding the indomitable Puffin. You know how he likes to buck from time to time for no reason? Well, he was having one of those sessions. As we approached the jump, he did a massive buck and at the same moment a pigeon flew up from behind the jump. He slapped on the anchors and veered out. I didn't have a chance and ended up unconscious on the ground having hit the jump wing head on."

"Oh my god. How absolutely ghastly."

"Anyway, the Baron came to the hospital with me in the ambulance and stayed until I regained consciousness."

"That was considerate."

"Yes, and what's more, he telephoned my mother and arranged for Rankin to pick her up each day so that she could be with me."

"Did he really do that?"

"Yes, and then when I was back and fit to ride, he made sure I hadn't lost my nerve by getting me back in the saddle straight away. Then he arranged for me to escort the disabled ride so that I didn't have time to worry about myself because I was too busy looking after the others. Without his help, I could easily have lost my career and my future."

"All very praiseworthy but are you sure he had not ear-marked you for Head Girl at that stage."

"No way, I already had a job lined up, so it was all altruistic."

"I didn't think he had it in him," mused Morien.

"Well, that's where you are wrong. I've seen him help others as well over the years. I've always thought of him as a caring person. He was so distraught when he lost his grandmother. Withdrew into his shell for months."

Working with Helen, Morien got to know her better and realised for the first time that she was engaged. Her fiancé was also involved with horses and was just branching out on his own as a racehorse trainer, not too far away at Newbury. Helen was truly excited about the prospect and looking forward to being completely absorbed in helping him when they married.

"I haven't told the Baron yet," she said, "I know I'm not indispensable but he does leave a lot to me, so I suppose I'd better give him reasonable notice to find a replacement."

"You'll leave an enormous gap," said Morien

"The ideal would be for my successor to work in tandem for a month. Perhaps you'd like to take it on"

"Me? No, no. I prefer the physical outdoor life."

"That's understandable but this work is very rewarding, and I do get to ride the more advanced horses each day. If you took the job on you would get the same privileges."

107

"An interesting thought, but I've still got lots to learn here." Changing the subject, she asked,

"Have you set the date for the wedding yet?" As she put the question, she realised that she had never been to a church wedding.

"No, but I'm hoping it will be in the next year," said Helen ruefully. "If he produces a few winners, we'll have the cash".

"I suppose it's an uncertain enterprise in the early days."

"Regretfully, yes."

"Does he let you ride the horses?"

"Sometimes. It's such a responsibility. Each one is worth thousands, and it only needs one pothole, a strained tendon or an upset tummy and all the work goes down the drain. A few missed race meetings can really interfere with a young horse's career."

"I've heard they racehorses as young as two years. Do you think that's right since they don't stop growing until four years old? They can hardly be strong enough, not much carrying muscle."

"Some are. But it takes careful muscle development. Balance is the biggest problem. But enough of me, would you do the Orders of the Day for me for tomorrow. I need to be with the vet this morning."

Morien was left to her own devices and loved it. Planning the day's jigsaw was such a challenge. When she came to Nina's name, she wondered cattily what nasties she could possibly devise for her. She had become more and more sure that Nina was her gremlin. It all fitted. Jealousy. There was no need for it but looking from Nina's point of view, Morien began to see. The Baron was spending an inordinate amount of his time with her and Merlin and she didn't think that his flirting with her had gone unnoticed by the others in the yard. Nina was blatantly smitten with the Baron, and he would be a good catch. Drago would obviously inherit the estate – the house, stables and vast acreage. What woman wouldn't love to live in that stately home and queen it over all her friends. A picture of Nina sprang to mind, teapot in hand, looking totally elegant. However, Morien was sure that it was money and image rather than the man that Nina wanted.

However, she didn't need to resort to such incredible bitchiness and cruelty to the horses. She obviously came from those horsy ranks that see animals as machines or a means to an end - fame and adulation. It was sad because she was a good rider and could jump the most terrifying obstacles without a blink. Morien wondered how the Baron could be so blind, but then she'd heard that love or was it sex, impeded the brain cells. She also recalled the Baron's remarks about planning permission. It seemed that perhaps he was just using the girl.

Musing, she realised that she could control Nina through the Orders of the Day. She laughed to herself as she decided to put Nina on the disabled ride. It was part of the compulsory coursework. There was a rota for this and looking back, Nina seemed to have missed her turns, probably to avoid brushing all the mud off the ponies. Morien giggled to herself at the image of Nina covered in dust and horsehairs. In the morning, she could lunge the young stock, another of the less popular jobs. That should keep her out of mischief.

She then arranged appointments with the farrier. Ten out of the forty needed some sort of attention. She checked the feed stocks which necessitated a trip to the feed rooms and barns to up-date the list for Helen. In the tack room, she found the saddlery repair book, but nothing needed mending. This was fun she thought as she returned to the office.

There was some correspondence from hopefuls applying for training places. She read through the letters and sorted and categorised them into possibles, hopeless and borderline then prepared replies for appointments to be organised. The morning rushed past, and she slipped out to see Merlin in her lunch break.

However, with Drago riding Merlin nearly every day, Morien missed her riding and the time for the results of the mare's pregnancy test was fast approaching. Her only highlight was the circus.

CHAPTER 19

As good as his word, Nathan sent her a note to meet him at the Land Rover. If seen, she was doing a vehicle check. With Rankin at the wheel, they managed to sneak away without detection. Morien felt like a naughty child out on a spree as she surveyed the outside world. It came to her that Drago was right, more than he realised. She had moved from one enclosed environment to another and this one was static and almost reclusive.

As they drove, the rolling hills rose majestically on the one side with the sea sparkling on the other. The traffic increased as they approached Chichester its old houses and narrow streets. What a place to explore thought Morien. She'd never had time in the past for such self-indulgence.

On the outskirts of the town was a large open park and it was here that they searched for a parking space. The sight of the circus with its big top already in place, the caravans and animal stalls, the noise of the generators, the smell of the sawdust set Morien's heart beating with excitement.

They soon found Gino, who seemed to have put on weight and looked particularly tubby and greasy haired. "My goodness, if it isn't young Morien." Gino looked her up and down, his eyes lighting salaciously at her lissom figure.

"Gino, I want you meet my new employer," She made the introductions. At first, Gino was quite casual.

"Hello, Nathan, long time no see. How's the world treating you? Got a place up the road I hear." Nathan smiled as Gino became quite obsequious when he found realised he was talking to an Earl. He obviously had never known Nathan's background when he was with the circus.

"Fell on your feet then," he growled, the intimacy of the group was not lost on him, and Morien could see the wheels turning in his brain as he made the wrong assumptions. Why was it she thought that everyone thought so badly of her?

"I wanted to see Renaldo," said Morien.

"That old codger," said Gino disparagingly. "He's past it these days. Time he went out to grass." Morien looked dismayed.

110

"Where will I find him?" she asked

"Try the lions. But he's more likely to be taking it easy with the horses."

"Hardly easy," muttered Morien as they made their way down to the stabling.

"Now I know why Renaldo got you out of here. Gino has turned into quite a nasty piece of work" commented Nathan as they found Renaldo with the horses. Morien hugged him ecstatically tears flowing with happiness.

"Hey, you're wetting my jacket," grumbled Renaldo laughing

"Getting to be a habit," murmured Nathan turning to Renaldo and exchanging pleasantries with much bantering.

"How are you, my old friend?"

"Mustn't grumble. Mustn't grumble."

The horses were being prepared for a practice session in the ring. Morien walked down the line admiring each occupant. They nuzzled her for carrots. A young girl, not much older than herself, was giving a final check to the harness.

"Come and watch," invited Renaldo as six liberty horses, all matching dapples, were led out and cantered into the Big Top with a man, wife and daughter team chatting enthusiastically as they circled the ring to the rowdy music. "History repeating itself." thought Morien.

The act was quite complicated, and Morien watched avidly trying to anticipate each sequence.

"Bring back memories?" queried Renaldo of the Earl

"It's been a long time," he responded "I haven't had the courage to come before. Bringing Morien was a good excuse, and it has helped to lay a few ghosts." Overhearing, Morien realised in her excitement how thoughtless she had been. The memories must be particularly painful but then, he had made the offer to bring her. Perhaps it was time for him to come to terms with things.

After watching for a while Renaldo could see the longing on Morien's face.

"Why don't you have a go for old time's sake? Give Nathan a treat."

"Do you think they'd mind?" Morien asked, anticipation written all over her.

111

"Let's ask," Renaldo called them over. "Rob, this is Morien. She and her father ran the liberties before you came."

"Oh yes, you auditioned us. Pleased to meet you again." The tall man took her hand.

"She would love to have a ride. What do you think?"

"Why not? The horses have worked now so they won't object to a newcomer," he said not knowing Morien's close connection to the animals.

"Oh, thank you," exclaimed Morien slipping out of her jacket and shoes. "I'd better go barefoot – these wouldn't be safe." Nathan watched her indulgently

"Going to give me a demonstration then?" he asked. Her shining eyes said it all.

Rob took the lead horse and Morien the second. The horse was strong and obedient. She was up, vaulting from side-to-side. Morien positively glowed as all the old sequences returned to her and then finally and triumphantly, she stood on the horse's rump as it cantered around the ring. Her thoughts turned to Drago. The old fire shot through her almost toppling her, but then it was replaced by a certain smugness.

"If only he could see me now, she thought gleefully. For all his training, I bet he'd fall off this one."

"Why don't you join us for the afternoon performance for old time's sake," suggested Rob,

"Do you really mean that?" Morien's eyes sparkled.

"Of course. Just look how well you fitted in. Anyway, it makes a change for us from the same old routine every day."

Tempted Morien gave in, and much fun took place developing a four routine and finding her a costume. Morien was in her element, while Renaldo and Nathan reminisced.

"She seems very happy," said Renaldo at last.

"In one way she is," responded Nathan "but there is a terrible friction with my son. He seems to almost deliberately misunderstand everything about her." He then launched into the chapter of disasters that seemed to follow Morien around.

"Sabotage," said Renaldo.

"What?"

"Sabotage. I know my girl. These things are impossible for her."

"Well, I must admit that I did wonder," commented the Earl

"You mean you did not trust her?" Renaldo was astounded. Nathan looked chastened.

"Over the years I've seen a lot of it here in the circus. The usual cause is jealousy."

Into the Earl's mind flashed Nina Blackthorpe-Smith who was being completely misled by his son. Was she thinking of wedding bells? He knew of Drago's ulterior motive regarding the building programme, but they did meet socially. Although Drago had had many girlfriends over the years Nina had a limpet quality about her. Allowing her to come on the course had probably been a big mistake. She was falling between two stools – not pupil material and not quite family.

The timing couldn't have been worse with the advent of Morien. Drago was so obviously intrigued. Morien was pretty, talented and rather mysterious and now he'd found the hidden horse.

With the competition on the horizon, they were spending many hours together. It was no wonder that Nina would be jealous. But would she sink so low.? If so, he certainly didn't want her in the family. His train of thought concerned him.

"Ah. I must admit that that could be part of the trouble. I think he's fallen for Morien but doesn't realise it. There's another student whom he's known for a long time. She has definitely set her cap at him. I wonder ." he trailed off musing.

"Well, you take care of her. I don't want her confidence destroyed or her heart broken. Morien is very special to me. She lost her mother when she was quite young, and her father was better at handling horses than human fillies."

"I'll remember. Without you she could have remained a mute. I'll look into things when I get home," promised Nathan and then, changing the subject "Isn't it time you retired my friend?"

"Huh. Why should I do that?"

"Old bones, old bones."

"What would I do, sit in some boarding house on my own? I have no family. This is my family and my friends."

"Yes, as long as you can work. Your boss seems more commercial than philanthropic."

Renaldo shrugged in response. "Well, he hasn't another clown to match me yet. Comedy is much harder than just being beautiful or clever."

113

"I agree and you were always good, but all that tumbling and intense physical stuff is very demanding."

"Well, I'm not ready for the scrap heap yet," snorted Renaldo.

"I'm not insinuating that you are, but I didn't like the attitude of that boss of yours. There was an underlying callousness." Again, Renaldo shrugged.

"When you're ready to retire I want you to come to me. No, no not for charity." he calmed Renaldo's protests. "I need help on the estate. I'm not so brisk as I used to be and need someone to share the load. Drago is completely involved with the horses." Renaldo looked interested.

"Promise you'll consider it when the time comes." Renaldo nodded his assent.

The matinee started. Nathan with Rankin had ringside seats. They clapped and laughed especially when the clowning Renaldo splashed water all over them. Then came the horses, with the graceful figure of Morien once more in spangles. She was completely in tune with the team and cameras flashed. Nathan felt that at least she had had some compensation for her past miseries, when she sat beside them glistening with more than sequins.

Gino found them after the show. "I'd forgotten how good you are," he congratulated Morien. "The whole act was raised a few notches and the crowd loved it." Morien smiled contentedly "Why don't you come back? I'll make it worth your while," he said persuasively.

Still glowing she wanted to laugh in his face.

"Too late," she murmured "Too late plus the fact that father always said 'never go back'"

Gino looked disappointed. "Anyway, I've got a good job and I like my work. It's different but similar and Merlin's doing very well." Gino looked cross.

"Oh well, I've work to do. Must get on." He nodded to the others and departed.

As they left Nathan asked Renaldo to come and spend the circus winter break at Wilton Hall.

"We need you," he said meaningfully "You can have your own place."

"Maybe, maybe but you just keep on looking after my little girl. Check for sabotage." They returned home in a cloud of happiness, so Nathan decided not to mention Nina with Morien that evening.

Several mornings later, Gill was reading the local rag. "Have you seen this picture?" she asked Morien. "Looks just like you," she laughed. Morien looked at the laughing girl on the horse. How ghastly, she hadn't noticed the photographers.

"I suppose there's a similarity," she conceded. "What's she doing?" she asked cagily

"Oh, some circus act, I think," said Gill turning the page.

That evening Morien surreptitiously secured the paper and hid it in her room. With any luck the Baron probably considered that such tabloids were beneath him. The very thought of him sent a thrill through her. She could visualise him recognising her picture with astonishment. Another criminal act to be added to her growing dossier.

CHAPTER 20

The strain between Morien and Drago was becoming increasingly difficult as the competition drew nearer. He teased her by constantly touching her when she least expected it, knowing he was playing on her emotions. It was like cat and mouse she thought recalling how he had caught her in his arms as she'd dismounted and then pretended to drop her. The tension was high although they both tried to eliminate it when working with Merlin. The horse really enjoyed the music and his paces improved visibly each day.

In the office, she tidied her desk and went to feed Merlin. To her surprise Drago was there, giving him a brush over. Morien could hardly believe her eyes. "Just creating a true rapport," commented the Baron "Nothing like a good massage." Morien looked away.

"I hoped you'd be around. I'd like you come to the next few sessions and check the overall performance of our creation."

Why was it that the huge loose box always seemed so small when he was in it?

"How's he going now?" she asked

"Like poetry between my legs," was the response, the horsy term taking on a different meaning from his lips. He regarded her, wary as usual.

"But to business. There's one combination that doesn't quite work. He finds the transitions difficult."

Companionably they leaned on the manger examining the programmed patterns they'd prepared, until Morien became aware that his attention was on her, not the paper. Over the several months since her arrival, she had become tanned and leaner. Her honey hair now streaked with sunshine. He put his hand on it gently trailing the strands through his fingers. She tensed but did not move.

"Why are you afraid of me?" he asked, gentling her again.

"I'm not," said Morien tossing her hair away from his roving fingers.

"Yes, you are. You're like a little shying unbroke."

"Maybe that's what I am."

"Oh, come off it."

116

"I thought we were sorting out the Kür."

"Back to safety again." He slipped his arm around her pinning her against the manger. "You know I want you. We get on really well when we talk about Merlin."

"Let's do just that then," muttered Morien desperately trying to extricate herself.

"No, not yet my beauty," he closed his mouth over hers ever so gently. She could feel the passion rising in her. Why not? cried her heart as his insistent tongue edged between her breathless teeth. Never, never had she been kissed like this - in fact, had she ever been kissed? She allowed herself to relax against him and felt the surge of his maleness, throbbing against her. As the kiss deepened, her response continued until she was all but wrapped around him. His hands travelled up and down her back, into her hair, igniting her. This was absolute rapture.

Slowly he lifted his head away, gazing at her fluttering eyelids. Bereft, she opened her eyes to find his smouldering into hers. For a stunned moment, they stared and then he kissed her again, this time with greater energy and insistence. He let his kisses flow around her ears, onto her neck. As she continued to respond he began to unfasten her blouse, kissing lower and lower until he found her hard peaked nipple. The exquisite agony of it made Morien gasp. Fire raced through every part of her. She wanted to cradle his head against her. Then something began gently to nag her deep down, causing her to push him away, even though she was completely star struck. It was wrong but she felt rapturous. She simply didn't know how to handle this. The callow youths of the circus and Gino's advances simply hadn't prepared her for such a tempest. Then images of Gino and his brutishness overtook her.

"So, the witch comes a little closer. You have a great aptitude for turning a guy on," he commented. "With your reputation though I don't know why I bother. Maybe it's to spite my father." he mused.

Suddenly the fire drained out of Morien's body, and she felt cold. Of course, he was just taunting her, making use of her and she regrettably had responded, allowing a chink in her armour. Anger surged as an immense feeling of rejection swept over her.

"I think Merlin wants his feed," she said gathering up the scattered papers from the manger. Realising that the horse was still hiding them from the door, Drago fiercely kissed her again, then turned and let himself out.

"I will come to the office later for you to re-hash the programme on paper. Arrange for yourself to be free for a schooling session tomorrow - of Merlin that is," he said with a parting smirk.

Morien leaned over the manger wondering if she was going to be sick. Here we go again she thought. Why do I let him do this to me? Where's my self-control, my self-respect? I'm getting like a bitch on heat.

Later in the office she couldn't concentrate. All the fun seemed to have gone out of the work and she was on tenterhooks waiting for him to appear. The part-time staff had gone home and Helen's absence added to the nightmare. She was still with the vet. sorting out a sick horse which was being taken to the Equine hospital. There would be no protecting buffer. The clock ticked.

When he eventually came, he slipped in quietly as she was on the phone and standing behind her began to massage her shoulders. Oh, the difficulty of continuing the conversation like an intelligent human being. Eventually she was able to hang up.

"You enjoy the office, don't you?"

"Yes," she said trying to escape from the chair where the firm hands held her in place. What was the use? She couldn't fight him. She didn't stand a hope. "I like the fascination of looking at the complications of the engine that runs the machine. It's rather like ." she sucked in her breath as the word 'circus' nearly slipped out.

"Rather like ..?" he waited expectantly.

"Oh nothing. What can I do for you?"

"Well, there's a leading question," he laughed.

Morien managed to escape from her chair and crossed the room ostensibly to get some blank paper, so that she could get the desk between them. Since her position was so fragile, she hardly dared tell him to keep his hands to himself.

"Right. Now where is the problem?" she asked. He outlined the sequence on the paper, humming the music for that portion.

"He seems to lose balance on the smaller circle so that when I ask for the long stride, the power is missing."

"We need another movement to engage the quarters." Morien toyed with her pencil. "Try a canter pirouette instead. He'll have his hocks well under."

As they talked Morien became more and more aware of Drago. He was like a regal lion, waiting to pounce.

"I really want to experiment with this now. It's lunch time so put the answer phone on and come to the school in ten minutes. When she arrived, he was already there loosening up Merlin.

Drago asked Morien to ride so that he could assess the new sequence. As the music started, Merlin lightened in anticipation and began to show off. As Morien restrained him, he dropped into piaffe, a high stepping trot on the spot.

"Well, you haven't seen this before," thought Morien encouraging the big horse to step higher and more rhythmically. Drago was transfixed to watch the ease of this difficult manoeuvre. With an imperceptible nudge, Morien pushed Merlin into the passage, a beautiful long striding, floating trot that appeared to be in slow motion. The Baron's face was a picture of amazement. Morien couldn't help feeling one up. However, she realised the musical cue was coming up, so she manoeuvred to be at the correct place in the arena for the new sequence. Merlin obediently dropped into walk and then answered her fresh requests.

The new moves were certainly much better suited to his physique, so he performed without hesitation or loss of balance.

"You never cease to amaze me," commented Drago "Whenever I've asked for passage and piaffe he loses rhythm."

"Maybe you're trying too hard. He doesn't need much. I sort of tuck my toes under his belly and push upwards. Anyway, the new steps seem to work."

"I wonder if we could introduce passage somewhere," mused the Baron.

"Maybe at the end, but let's get everything else right first." Morien was nothing if not practical.

They swapped places. With Drago in the saddle, Morien went to rewind the music. She was more than a little amused to see Drago attempting the advanced paces. Merlin was not so much on his toes as he'd been with Morien, so all the responses were slower and less sparkling. Becoming aware of her gaze the Baron sent the horse forward and began to work on the routine.

119

The day of the competition dawned, and Morien was up extremely early to bath and plait Merlin for the show. "This is your big day," she told him, "I want you to remember how good you are and do everything right." His coat glistened and he look so smart. She felt a small pang when she remembered the decorations he would have worn at the circus. His colouring would have set them off so well.

She started plaiting with practised hand working quickly. Merlin kept shuffling. "Stand still your naughty boy or I might stick a needle in you." Soon a smart row of tiny coils appeared. Not a hair out of place. Then Morien plaited his tail, using swift underhand twists, drawing the lose hair from the side at each turn. This ended in a long pigtail that she looped up and stitched neatly in place.

"There, all the plaits in. You do look good." She gave him the final once over then went to prepare Iatro. Despite the hold-up in his training, the Baron was taking him since the horse had qualified earlier in the year. He was still entered in other classes. He'd been plaited the night before because he was used to all the fuss and didn't get into a mess. Morien groomed him and checked him for any stains.

She dressed both horses in their travelling gear ready to load on the lorry and then went to fetch Helen who had been finishing off all the office work and posting the notices. It was still only 7.00 a.m.

"All set," she said.

"Great, just coming."

Together they boxed the two horses making everything secure. Gill appeared in a rush as usual. She had been doing all the mucking out for Morien and Helen leaving them free. Duties over, she joined them just as they were about to leave. Nina was noticeable by her absence. She had done everything in her power to be involved but Drago had flattered her out of it by offering to drive her to the show himself, so she obviously hadn't bothered to get out of bed. Thus, Morien and Gill travelled the horses with Helen driving. The height of the lorry gave Morien a super view of the surrounding countryside. She was so excited. Soon they found themselves joining a queue with other lorries and trailers making their way into the showground.

The showground was enormous, the dressage event - although international - being only a small part of this County extravaganza. Morien was amazed drinking in all the activities. There was a large press tent, and several television crews were busy setting up. Qualified horses had come from all over the country and some from abroad to enter the horse competitions.

"Wow, this is incredible, so vast."

"Yes, this is one of the permanent County showgrounds," said Helen. "Not only horses but all manner of country pursuits."

"Haven't you ever been to one?" Gill asked Morien.

"Gosh, no, "Morien exclaimed.

They were directed to the horse lines where there were a few other early birds like themselves. They pulled up and then lowered the ramp to allow the horses more ventilation and to accustom them to the noises.

"Gill, you stay here and look after the boys while we go and register," said Helen. As she smoothed out the showground plan and located their position and that of the secretary's tent. "Over that way, I think" she pointed out the way. They headed for the competition office to register their arrival, hand in their music tapes and collect the competition numbers. They found some signposts but still had a longish walk.

Helen seemed to know everybody. Several ladies were busy in the office sorting numbers and entry forms. One was pinning large sheets onto easels listing the horses in the various events with start times for each horse. Morien and Helen noted down their times.

"Tell us about Drago's new horse," requested a chap in a bowler looking at the entry lists. "He seems rather young for the Kür the at this level."

"The Baron knows what he's doing," Helen responded. "The horse has lots of potential."

"Where did he find him?" asked another

"Well, when Iatro was injured his hopes faded. This horse is a livery at the yard." They hastily made their escape.

"Come on," said Helen "let's explore the arenas where we'll be competing later." Since it was early, there were no judges in situ. Merlin and Iatro were involved in two competitions in two different arenas which Helen and Morien walked over carefully looking for small dips and bumps that might put the horses off their stride and rhythm. The area chosen for the Kür was perfect, like a bowling green.

"There will be five judges on this arena," said Helen "so no one can fudge their movements. They will be viewed from all possible angles. See that electronic board over there? It will be displaying the points for each judge for each horse." Morien was overawed by the scale.

Back at the horsebox they unloaded the horses. With Gill's help they spruced them up to show condition with stencilled patterns on their quarters and shining oiled hooves. Morien decided to lunge Merlin who was being very skittish.

"Once he's settled, tack him up and ride quietly around letting him look at everything," advised Helen.

"How long have we got before the first test?" asked Morien.

"About an hour," said Helen looking at her watch, "so start warming him up half an hour before."

"OK"

"I wonder where the Baron is. He's usually here by now." Helen was obviously beginning to get worried. The Baron was such a stickler for being early and relaxed so as not to upset the horses with personal emotions.

Morien took Merlin to the exercise area. There were several other horses being lightly lunged so he didn't keep looking back towards the lorry lines. He soon settled and began to work through well from behind in a balanced manner. When he was nicely loosened up, she tacked him up and rode out amongst all the noise and sights. Merlin was reasonably well behaved, only spooking a little at all the new sights. Paper bags blowing around were the main hazard, since they appeared so unexpectedly. When they arrived back at the exercise area Helen was loosening up Iatro.

"The Baron's still not arrived," she called over. "Gill's gone to phone. You and I will have to ride if he doesn't make it." Morien looked surprised.

"Don't changes of rider matter?"

"No. It's the horse that's registered," said Helen "Do you know the test? I'll call it out for you as Iatro goes about 15 minutes before Merlin."

"I've ridden bits of it and seen it often enough."

At the last competition, she had seen callers at work. It needed a fair bit of skill to advise the rider of what was coming next, in time for them to prepare and perform, without saying more than they could assimilate at one time. Also, it needed a clear carrying voice. It was immensely valuable because it allowed the rider to concentrate on producing good results from the horse without becoming tense and worried about forgetfulness.

It would be great to ride her horse herself, she thought and secretly hoped that the Baron would not make it.

CHAPTER 22

He didn't. He was now three hours late. Helen had finished on Iatro who had given a good showing considering his lay-off. She quietly explained the principles of the test to Morien, taking her through the sequences.

"Just relax. I will call out the test for you so you can focus on Merlin. Just show off all his paces to the judge. As long as you change pace at the right place and give his best effort, that's all there is to it." What an understatement!

So, Morien found herself riding into the arena to commence her first ever dressage test and in an international competition.

"Who cares," she thought "This is nothing compared with the circus." Merlin co-operated completely and as he began to flow, she wanted to sing with happiness. The big horse swanked throughout, right up to the final salute - a true showman. As they left the arena, Morien noticed that quite a few people had come to watch.

"Wow" exclaimed Helen greeting her at the exit. "They're going to have difficulty finding fault with that."

Morien was exploding with pride as they walked back to the horsebox.

"You didn't seem a bit nervous."

"I wasn't." said Morien "It was such fun only having to produce the right movements." No audience to please, she thought to herself. Helen gave her a quizzical look.

Several people who had followed them to get a closer look at Merlin started chatting to Helen.

"Nice horse," commented on woman "Didn't realise it was one of Drago's."

"You know Sabrina is looking for a new Olympic horse, don't you?" said another.

"I don't think he's for sale at the moment," responded Helen "but keep in touch."

"I'd be interested if Drago puts a price on him," said a be-spurred young man. To Morien "You rode him nicely."

"The horse is a livery but give me a ring at the office and I'll let you know," said Helen.

Morien was stunned. Merlin wasn't and never would be for sale. He was obviously only horseflesh and money to all these people - not a friend, a joy.

"What's going on?" she muttered in Helen's ear.

"Never turn down a good offer," said Helen brightly then looking a Morien meaningfully she said, "You might need to sell him at some point."

Just then Gill returned and interrupted any further discussion as they untacked the horses.

"The queue for the phone was a mile long," she complained. "They said at the Hall that he'd left hours ago." she announced.

"What on earth has happened to him?" queried Helen by now she was getting really worried. With two horses to prepare for the Kür, time was running out. The Baron always liked to explore the venue, examine the finer points of the arena looking for uneven spots and to generally get the feel of a place before a competition. He always, always rode for a least 20 minutes before entering an arena. Where on earth could he be?

Morien, on the other hand, was revelling in his absence. The results of the earlier event were up on the board, and she had come second. Second in her first high-level competition. Suddenly she knew that this was what she wanted to do with her life. She wanted to breed and train horses for the dressage arena, to maximise their beauty through perfect paces.

Then a frission of fear ran through her as she remembered the axe hanging over her head. If Merlin had succeeded in his one night of love, she would be out on her ear with no future at all. She decided to join Helen and Gill who were anxiously scanning the showground.

"Congratulations on your result." Gill clapped her on the shoulder. "This game is obviously your cup of tea."

"Yes, well done," conceded Helen. "I think we'd better start preparing these two for the Kür. The Baron is sure to be here shortly and then he can take over, even at the shortest notice. This event means so much to him." Gill helped them get organised and mounted.

"I'm going to watch the show jumping for a while," she announced, "I'll keep my eye open for the Baron and tell him where you are."

"Thanks" said Helen moving Iatro towards the riding in area. For the next little while both riders were in deep concentration, preparing their horses. Then Helen joined Morien.

"Still no sign," she said dejectedly. "All those endless hours of training, all gone to waste." She looked completely disconsolate. Morien nodded scanning the crowds.

"How well do you know Iatro's Kür?" she asked. Helen looked startled.

"Not at all. I just haven't been around."

"Couldn't you just invent something?"

"Absolutely not. I'm going to the secretary's tent to withdraw them," she said with finality.

"Withdraw Iatro if you want but I'm going to ride Merlin." Helen looked aghast.

"This is the very top level in the country," Helen explained "Most of the entries are Olympic standard or equivalent."

"I don't care," said Morien nonchalantly "You said earlier that it's the horse that entered not the rider."

"Yes, but ."

"But nothing. This is my horse and I know the routine backwards." Helen looked completely nonplussed.

"She's absolutely right," said a voice behind them. Unnoticed during their heated discussion the Baron had arrived ---- on crutches!!

"What on earth has happened." dismounting, the girls were all concern.

"Crashed the car! Explanations can wait. It's obvious I can't ride today. Scratch Iatro if you don't want to ride him and you - you get going and don't let me down." They both wanted to ask questions, but his attitude silenced them. Morien backed off and mounted Merlin, wheeling away to take her mind off this disturbing man. Now she was riding with his permission. No one could take that away.

When her entry time was due, she walked Merlin to the vicinity of the Kür arena. Seating on three sides, packed to capacity, surrounded it. There in the front row was the Baron with Rankin and the Earl. He gave her the thumbs up as the previous horse finished and left the arena. Now it was her turn. Butterflies began to flit in her stomach, so she leaned forward and whispered in Merlin's ear to regain her confidence.

"This is for Dad, Merlin. For all the magic moments that he'd planned for you. Let's make his legacy, an offering of joy."

Merlin flicked his ears and she felt him grow beneath her as he took in the crowds. They circled outside waiting for their music to start and then there it was - the cue. Morien turned Merlin into the arena and started the Kür.

There was no doubt. Merlin was on the top of his form, completely attentive and rhythmical, literally dancing through all the most difficult manoeuvres as though he was made of thistledown. As they approached the final sequence Morien knew that he was ready to offer her the piaffe and passage, which were not in the routine but went well with this part of the music. After all, it was freestyle. She asked the question and Merlin promptly responded in the most brilliant manner. As they came to the final halt and salute, Morien knew that they had given the most magnificent performance of their lives.

The crowd clapped quietly as she turned to leave the arena. When they realised that Merlin was not upset by the noise, they all came to their feet for a standing ovation, unheard of in such exclusive circles. People surrounded them, patting Merlin as though he had just won the Derby and was heading for the winners' enclosure. He loved it. "I'll give you whatever you ask for that horse." The man who'd shown interest earlier pushed his card in her hand. "Give me a ring tomorrow."

"Not so fast, I want this one for Sabrina."

"Outbid me then," smiled the man departing.

"Please give me first refusal won't you." The woman wrote her address on a scrap of paper and gave it to Morien.

"But he's not for sale," gasped Morien, confused by this bizarre behaviour.

"Every horse has a price." The woman smiled knowingly giving Helen the wink.

Eventually, they fought their way back to the horse lines and Morien dismounting gave him some carrots.

"That was just so beautiful, Morien. You and your horse have such talent. It was right that you should have had a chance to prove it. I've never, not never, seen a standing ovation before." Helen made a fuss of Merlin.

"I'm just so happy because we fulfilled my father's dream." Morien's eyes shone. "He always said Merlin had the best paces and temperament of any he'd bred. I only wish he could have lived to see today."

"When are you going to tell us all about him?" questioned Gill "Surely you don't have to be so secretive. Have you committed some gruesome crime?" They all laughed.

"Don't push her, Gill. Some people prefer to be private. They don't wear their lives on their sleeves."

"Oh well, I'm so ordinary I have to talk about it to convince myself I exist," Gill responded.

"I don't think you'd better box Merlin yet. You have to go to the prize giving for the first competition and for the second - who knows ----"

"Gosh, do we have to ride?"

"Only at major event like this - for the benefit of the sponsor and TV," said Helen

"How did Iatro make out this morning's test?" asked Morien feeling guilty for having completely forgotten the other horse and rider.

"We only made seventh place," said Helen "just out of the ribbons. But I'm pleased with him seeing he was out of training."

"I think that's particularly good because you have not been riding much lately either."

"Let's go. The Baron said to meet him near arena one." They walked down together leading Merlin, leaving Iatro safely boxed in the lorry with a feed.

The glow on Drago's face said it all. "You've won, my dear," he smiled his magic all- enveloping smile.

"Not only won but won by the biggest margin of all time. My hand is worn out from receiving congratulations on your behalf and half the county wants to buy him."

Morien bristled and withdrew. Fear caught her again. Why was everyone talking about buying her horse?

"I'm truly delighted that we did so well and that your reputation is suitably enhanced."

His face clouded. "You'd better teach your poule some manners," he threw at his father, turning his back on her.

"Go and get your prize, Morien," said the Earl. "You've earned it on all counts." She nodded and vaulted onto Merlin as her name was called.

To her surprise, with the rosette was quite a large cheque and it was made out in her name not the Baron's. For the first time, she would be above the breadline.

The Baron was very much involved with all his cronies when she came out of the ring and getting Merlin home was Morien's priority, so they were soon on the road.

Helen had some details of the car crash. "It seems a dog ran out from the verge and in avoiding it, the car went down a small embankment. Nina's got some facial injuries - not too bad - and whiplash and Drago strained his sacro-ileac and bruised both knees. They were lucky." Morien's thoughts about Nina were not kind.

They were all pretty tired when they got back and by the time they had settled the horses, showers and food were paramount. However Helen said "We'd better just check and lock up the office," Morien followed reluctantly. Helen opened the post which lay still untouched from the morning. She wanted news from the Equine College on the sick horse, Stardust, but it seemed there was no news.

Morien became aware that Helen had become very still, frowning at the letter in her hand.

"Bad news?" queried Morien, her thoughts on Stardust. Silently, Helen handed her the letter. At first, she was too tired to take in the contents and then realisation dawned. The letter was about the Baron's special mare. The pregnancy test was positive!!!

The joys of the day became a numb memory. Her tiredness took over as the tears began to fall. Helen tried to comfort her, but Morien huddled in her misery.

"I'll have to leave," she whispered. "But where, where will I go?" the despair was too apparent. Momentarily fear took over and she began to shake.

"Don't be silly," said Helen firmly handing her some tissues. "I'm sure it won't come to that."

"Of course, it will. In his eyes, I'm a series of catastrophes waiting to attack his horses. Since my arrival he must live in horror about what he will find each day when he enters the yard."

So now again all her life was in ruins. She would have to leave. He'd never forgive her for having spoiled his mare's breeding programme. It was all so unfair. For dressage Merlin was probably better suited than all the rest of the unsuccessful stallions put together, but she could never confess. She was bound by her promise. Nathan must help her. Surely he could think of something otherwise she would have to face reality and sell Merlin.

Life was grossly unfair. She would now never have another chance like todays. All those dreams at the competition of breeding and competing on beautiful horses were only that, dreams, dreams of an audacious child above her station. She felt for the business cards and the scrap of paper in her pocket. Fate dealt cruel blows.

"What kind of money would I get for Merlin?" she raised her tearstained face to Helen.

"Well into five figures after today's performance," she responded.

"You mean £10,000?" Morien looked stunned.

"More like £50k," was the reply as the 'phone rang.

"Yes … yes. There was some post. No … no news of Stardust. The test result – um – er – yes – positive." There was a silence which drew out, then " Yes, yes, she' here with me. I've just told her. ….. OK, all right." She hung up.

"He wants to see you – now – and would you take the letter." Helen came around the desk and took the sobbing Morien in her arms.

"It's going to be OK."

"How can you say that? Apart from using Merlin to get himself out of a fix, he has no time for me."

"Listen, if the worst comes to the worst my fiancé could use you as a groom although we couldn't pay to start with. But it would be a roof over your head for you and Merlin. He's not too far away, about 50 miles as the crow flies."

"Oh Helen." Such generosity was so unexpected.

" Go now. Be strong. His bark is much worse than his bite."

Dragging her feet, Morien made her way to the house. She could do with a bath and some sleep but quite frankly who cared. She had been summoned. The stress and tension that she had been under for the last few weeks was beginning to take its toll and she felt depression starting to take the upper hand. Renaldo had given her a tremendous gift arranging for her to come here and she, through apparent carelessness, had thrown it all away.

Kind though Helen's offer was, a racing yard was hardly the place for Merlin beyond a temporary arrangement. Because of his dressage ability, Wilton Hall had turned out to be such a perfect place for both of them. He enjoyed his work and should be in a home where he could advance to the highest levels. And now, it had all gone wrong. She had been systematically undermined – destroyed.

It would not have been so bad if she had been the femme fatale that some had labelled her because then she would truly have been in competition with Nina and might well have won this imaginary war. She knew that the Baron was attracted to her on a physical level and also knew that she could have exploited this if it had been her nature. But she was totally misunderstood on all fronts, innocent of any ulterior motives. That was half of her trouble, she was too innocent. As a consequence, she was irresistibly enamoured with the Baron. She couldn't seem to control her emotions when in his presence, so it truly looked as though she wore her heart on her sleeve. What a fool!! Was there something wrong with her that this was the second job she was losing because of a man?

How was she going to survive out there in the real world? She hadn't done very well so far. She was desperately trying to remember who had made the best offer for Merlin. It was now quite clear to her that her horse was a liability. She could hardly expect Lady Luck to favour her twice and provide them both with a home. She recalled the man looking for an Olympic horse for one of the team members. Was it right that Morien should deny Merlin such opportunities and fame? Her heart ached as she found herself at the house.

CHAPTER 23

Bracing herself and drawing herself up to her full elfin height she entered the room and stood back against the closed door, letter in hand. Her heart jerked. The Baron was standing with near the fire.

"May I see the letter," said Drago. He seemed imperious and distant as she walked over to him.

"Ironic isn't it," he said as he took it from her. "All those trips to top stallions, all that expense, all for nothing. She simply would not take." He looked up and fixed her eyes. "Then one night of abandoned love and she fell." Morien blushed to the roots of her hair.

"Perhaps we could get it aborted," she returned.

"Oh, do you have experience of such matters?" Again, the double entendre, it was so insulting. She turned away. "Anyway, it would be too risky at this stage."

"I'm truly sorry."

"There are some things that we have to live with. Your stallion does have all the attributes necessary in a dressage horse as today's results have shown. He generated a lot of interest." He caught a flash of pride in her eyes before she lowered them and looked away. "I was really frustrated not having had the chance to ride him."

"Your loss was my gain," said Morien momentarily remembering.

"Yes, at least there is something that you do well." His irony was not lost on her. "I wish we knew more about his breeding. He is quite a remarkable horse, a stallion with superb movement and an excellent temperament to go with it. The foal will be intriguing knowing how well the mare stamps her stock. Did it never cross your mind to wonder why I didn't get the vet straightaway?"

"You mean that there was a possibility that the pregnancy could have been averted?"

"Yes, there are drugs nowadays."

"But you didn't. You wanted this foal." He smiled and nodded "What had I to lose?"

"I cannot believe this. I have been on tenterhooks. I've hardly slept or eaten, terrified of there being a positive result and all the time you have been gloatingly waiting for the good news." Morien was beside herself feeling she had nothing to lose. She wanted to physically hit him for his lack of understanding and consideration. What a self-centred creature! The Baron looked taken aback.

"I see it all now. This was a form of punishment. How sadistic. I suffer and you gain. Why do you need to treat me so badly? You must have had a rotten insecure childhood to make you such a monster." Her green eyes flashed and sparkled with anger.

"My, my, what a harridan." With a smile, he pretended to back away aware of her clenched fists.

"To think I came here this evening feeling responsible for destroying your breeding programme, prepared to give up all that I'd worked for including my security just to find that you had been playing with me."

"That is where you are wrong. You have been playing with me and with my father. Your so-called security was getting your talons into him and hanging on."

"I think it is time I left, and I will be taking Merlin with me." Morien swung her head defiantly. Did he dare call her bluff? Let him try.

"It will be a relief for all of us. Since you arrived our lives have been visited with disaster after disaster. I hardly dare go down to the yard for fear of your next exploit."

"Your problem is that you're not interested in the truth," she flung at him.

"Truth? What do you know about truth? It's clear you know more about your horse than you are letting on."

"Maybe I do, but it's none of your business."

"If that's your attitude, go!"

As she strode for the door trying desperately to maintain her dignity, Nathan had just appeared and was party to the last bit of the conversation. "Indeed, she does." Nathan intervened, blocking her exit. "What's all this rowing about?"

"So, there are secrets and, just as I thought, I'm the one in the dark." Drago eyed her maliciously and then glowered at the Earl.

133

"There is just <u>one</u> secret that I asked Morien to keep because of your massive prejudice."

"And what might that be? Dislike of your licentious life and seduction of young ladies?"

"I think it's about time you dropped that stance with me," said Nathan severely. "You have now seen with the evidence of your own eyes and your own backside whilst sitting on the animal, a horse trained exclusively, together with its rider, in the tradition of the circus."

Drago looked stunned and then the anger exploded "I don't believe you." His fury surged around the room.

"You recognised this child's talent from the first moment you saw her ride. Yes, I acknowledge you have taught her, and she has been an exceptionally quick study but she was already well on the way and had a deep understanding of how to communicate with a horse so that it could respond correctly." The Baron turned away

"I would also remind you that when you found us training that morning, you couldn't wait to sit on the horse and explore its development. We all know what happened after that. You can't kid me that you were only riding Merlin because Iatro was lame. There was much more to it than that."

Morien watched the various realisations flitting over the Baron's face but could see that he still did not wish to acknowledge the matter, especially since he felt he had been duped.

"Morien came to us through my old circus friend, Renaldo, because on the accidental death of her father she was left destitute. At that time, her only alternative to finding a place that would take her and her horse was to become the circus owner's mistress." The Baron's lip curled. "Knowing of your unshakable prejudice towards anything connected with the circus, we decided, to protect her from your attitude, it would be in her best interests to overlook her history to ensure her place here." Drago shrugged.

"Your unexpected rudeness and unkind assumptions that she was my mistress took us both by surprise and I dreaded to think how you would have treated her had you known the whole truth." Drago looked momentarily nonplussed. Morien thought perhaps he was embarrassed, recalling his insulting behaviour.

134

"I thought that that was a temporary misunderstanding," continued Nathan, "and that you would soon realise your error. But I can see now that that was not the case. In reality, she is like a daughter to me. It has been doubly hard for her since someone has been cruelly undermining her."

Drago was glaring at Nathan. "Always her champion," his scorn surfacing.

Morien cringed. "So, now that you know the truth, I don't feel I can stay any longer accepting your training under false pretences." She didn't wait for his reaction and marched towards the door. As she went, she heard Drago's cold words to his father, "The circus killed my mother."

Retreating to her room she felt totally dejected, as the horror of those words began to penetrate. The coldness, the bitterness they contained was immense. His dislike of the circus was much more than training methods or useless itinerants. There was no way she could stay now. Drago had not dismissed her nor confirmed that she could stay. In fact, she was quite unsure of what his feelings were apart from pleasure about the foal. She had taken the initiative, had just burnt her boats and the enormity of it flowed over her. She knew, however, that she was right. The nastiness of Nina, the friction with the Baron had made her life intolerable and she was far too obligated to the Earl. Every day seemed more stressful than the one before. She was losing weight faster than she could afford. She simple couldn't be ill. Where could she go? Her thoughts churned endlessly, chasing away any chance of sleep.

As she tossed from side to side suddenly, she remembered the cheque she'd won. Together with the pocket money she'd earned so far, she could survive for a while without selling Merlin. Fortunately, she'd had to open a bank account for her wages when she'd first arrived. So, what was she hanging about for? She would go to Helen's fiancé near Newbury. After all the offer had been genuinely made.

CHAPTER 24

No time like the present. With that thought she climbed out of bed and packed her meagre belongings.

Quietly she let herself out and made her way to the tack room for Merlin's gear. At this time of night, there was no one about as she entered Merlin's box and tacked him up. Feeling only slightly guilty about the untidy stable, she mounted and rode out heading across the parkland to the main gate, a grey moving shadow in the moonlight. At the gates, she paused, remembering the awe of that first day.

Then stiffening her resolve, she set off down the road. She only had a vague idea of which way she was going but felt that people would help. She only had to ask. At that moment, she simply wanted to put a good distance between herself and Wilton Hall. Memories of Drago, his style, his arrogance, dragged at her heart but she pushed them away.

When dawn broke, they were well out into the countryside. Helen had said the yard was to the north over the downs. Morien had been following the stars until the sunrise helped her to orientate herself. It was red, heralding rain so she thought she should try to find a livery yard for Merlin to rest. They had been travelling for two hours up into the hills. It took a further two hours to find a village by which time the heavens had opened and they were both drenched. Morien waylaid a pedestrian who directed her to a livery yard. She dismounted and entered the yard to be greeted by a plump rather scruffy looking woman.

"Have you a stable to rent?" she asked hesitantly. The woman eyed her suspiciously.

"You're not local," she said.

"No, I'm having a riding holiday," lied Morien "We're soaked, and my horse needs a rest."

"Yes, I've got an empty box. It'll be £15 per day, food extra." Morien gasped. She really hadn't thought this through. She needed a bed for herself – what would that cost? Still there was no choice, she would have to get that cheque cashed quickly.

"OK" she said as the woman began to make a fuss of Merlin.

"Nice horse. Tie him up over there and we'll put down a bed." Between them they spread a good layer of straw and filled water buckets and a hay net.

"By the way, I'm Doreen," said the woman. "Where have you come from?"

"Oh, down south," responded Morien

"Far?"

"We've been on the road for five days," answered Morien who had no idea of distances.

"Where're you heading?"

Morien covered herself "Well, we've got another ten days so wherever we end up in two or three will be the end, since we need time to head back." Doreen seemed to accept her yarn. She also recommended a few addresses for bed and breakfast.

"I'll see you later." Morien headed for the village centre to find a bank. There she was informed that the cheque would take at least five days to clear. She wasn't far enough away to be safe if the Baron came looking for her and with her accessible meagre savings, she couldn't afford five days' expense. One night was the longest. Drawing out what little cash she had, she went in search of some overnight accommodation. The village seemed full of B & Bs obviously relying on summer tourists, so she easily found a place near to the yard. Then totally exhausted, she fell asleep to nightmares of a rampaging Baron sending out the "furies" to find her.

Later after a quick fish and chip supper she went back to Merlin who seemed content enough. Doreen, however, was not.

"You didn't tell me he's a stallion," she said angrily. "I've had to turn all my mares out in the paddock down the other side of the farm. He was busy serenading them."

Morien was dismayed. Here I go again, she thought, causing upset. "He's very well mannered, "she protested.

"Well, I couldn't take the risk." said Doreen crossly. "How could I be sure?"

"Please let him stay," begged Morien "Just till tomorrow. I promise we'll leave early."

"Well, the mares are out now so one night won't make a difference," said Doreen grudgingly. "But off first thing, do you hear? and," she added "just pray it doesn't rain again giving me

137

wet horses in the morning that can't be ridden by my customers."
She disappeared into the buildings.

Morien stayed with Merlin for a while. Why was life giving
her such a bad deal? She had wanted so much to be part of the
life and business of Wilton Hall. It had offered so much and was
the perfect environment for Merlin. She remembered her futile
dreams of the training and breeding programmes. Drago, she
thought, had everything except, apparently, the ability to enjoy it
with grace. She leaned against Merlin, taking comfort from the
only unargumentative friend that she had.

The following morning, she went to examine a map she'd seen
on the bus shelter and, to her relief, a road to Newbury was
shown, so at least she now had a proper route to follow. At the
stables, she settled up with Doreen – thankfully it hadn't rained
– tacked up and left.

The morning was bright, no sign of further rain. The
landscape stretched flat all around them making the going easy.
By lunch time, they found an area of open grassland with a
stream where Morien watered Merlin and let him rest and graze.
She had nothing but she didn't care as she lay back in the heather
and explored the sensation of absolute freedom, just like the
skylarks singing overhead. The birdsong, the bees murmuring in
the heather, the trickling of the stream, the munch, munch,
munch from Merlin, brought total contentment.

Soon, however, they were en route again, and Morien was
relieved to find a pub which, to her delight, had a hitching rail
outside. Standing at the bar waiting for her lemonade and
sandwich she became aware of the radio in the background. It
seemed to be a local news broadcast. Her heart stopped as she
heard a report of the dressage competition. The interviewer was
asking lots of questions and it came out that the grey stallion was
now missing from Wilton Hall. They'd be interested to hear of
its whereabouts. Momentarily she was transfixed. Then
glancing around, she realised that no one else was listening.

Now what did she do? She couldn't be that far from the racing
yard, but would Derek take her in now? She beat a hasty retreat.
How could Drago do this to her? It made her sound like a petty
horse thief, yet Merlin was hers. Now she was truly a fugitive.
Somehow she had to find her way without being seen by too
many people. She looked at her hand-drawn map. The dual

carriageway stood out. Several miles of straight road which would leave her very exposed. But with any kind of luck, she could have a good gallop down the verge and reduce the overall distance considerably. She decided to take the risk.

There it was. The verge was extremely wide, so she asked Merlin to really stretch. He loved it and simply powered along. She wondered if he'd missed his vocation and would make a better racehorse. They covered about five miles, and he was beginning to tire. As they slowed down to a walk, she noticed that he was limping a little. Dismounting, she discovered one of his shoes had come loose and twisted slightly, pressing on the sensitive part of his foot. Once more disaster had struck. Without tools, she couldn't remove the shoe. There was nothing for it, she'd have to find a farrier – but where?

She trudged disconsolately along leading Merlin, looking for a turn-off to a village, her fears of being recognised increasing by the minute. It was some time before they found a side road with Merlin's limp becoming more pronounced. As the road narrowed, she found she was holding up a land rover which was waiting to overtake. Once around the bend the vehicle passed her and then pulled up. The driver got out, a tall, ruddy faced man with muddy boots.

"You look as though you're in trouble," he said, "Your horse has quite a limp".

"You can say that again," responded Morien. "I need a farrier."

"Let's have a look," he lifted Merlin's hoof. "Hmm," he mused "not something I can handle. The blacksmiths are mostly itinerant round here, travelling to the horses as you might say." Morien's heart sank.

"Tell you what, he shouldn't walk any further. You stay here and I'll get my daughter to bring the trailer over and we'll sort you out." With a wave and a smile, he drove off.

"So," thought Morien, "knights of the road still do exist. What a charming man – not like someone she could think of. Why did Drago invade her thoughts unmercilessly? Each time he flashed into her mind; her stomach churned. Waiting here on the roadside, she felt like a sitting duck. Anyone could see her and report back. Then nervously, she wondered if the farmer had recognised her and perhaps his intentions were not honourable at

139

all. Ah well, she had nothing more to lose. If the trailer never came at least they were having a rest.

But the trailer did come. An obviously horsey girl greeted her as she pulled up and lowered the ramp on the trailer. Between them they loaded Merlin and Morien climbed into the passenger seat.

"I 'phoned the farrier and you're in luck. He's in the area and said he'd get to our place some time after lunch."

"I don't know how I can thank you." said Morien

"It's nothing. I think I'm destined for rescue work. I always get called out if there's a horse problem on the road. My name's Isobel by the way, Iso for short. What's yours?"

"Morien"

"So, Morien, how do you come to be riding alone in this neck of the woods?" Morien had to continue her fabrication.

"I'm on a riding holiday. I'm alone 'cos my friend backed out at the last minute."

"Quite some horse you've got."

"Yes, he's quite a star." Then she had an idea that could throw people off the trail. "He's actually a circus horse and this is our resting period. Because during the season he is cooped up and travelling in trailers all the time, I thought he'd enjoy the open road."

"And does he?"

"Absolutely."

"Does he like performing?"

"Oh yes. We have a troupe of six." Morien went on to describe the life she'd led with her father.

"I've never met a circus horse before. What a thrill."

By the time they arrived at the farm with its many outbuildings, Morien and Iso were firm friends. Iso told her about the three competition horses she owned.

They unloaded Merlin and put him in a large airy stable with food and water to await the farrier.

CHAPTER 25

Morien looked around her. "Quite a place you've got here," she said.

"Yes, we've got about 100 acres. Dad farms sheep mainly so there's some land available for my horses. Come and meet them." Iso then took her further down the yard.

"They are beautiful," said Morien, "and really well muscled."

"I'm an event rider," said Iso, " so they've got to be really fit."

"I never really understood about eventing," said Morien. Iso looked surprised then laughed. "I suppose the circus is rather a closed world." she went on to explain. "Eventing is a three-discipline sport for horses over one or three days. The first phase is the dressage, the second cross-country jumping and the third the show jumping."

"Gosh, that sounds like a contradiction, each bit needing a different muscle development."

"I guess you're right. Hadn't thought of that. "Iso looked at her curiously. "But it's more fun than just doing one bit. Anyway, I'm just going to loosen up Charlie and work on his dressage. Want to come?"

"You bet," said Morien. A whole new world had suddenly opened up. There hadn't been any horses in training at Wilton Hall specifically for eventing, so it had never been discussed in any detail. There was a cross-country course but training on it had been later in the curriculum of the WP course. As they tacked up Charlie, a seventeen-hand dark bay, gelding, Iso told Morien of various competitions she'd been to and the rosettes she'd won. "Somehow though, I can't get that elusive win to qualify for the nationals."

They went out to the outdoor manege and Iso started to work Charlie. Morien found herself running a critical eye over his conformation and paces. Her months at Wilton Hall had not been wasted. Although she was not the skinny type, Iso was particularly tall, so her legs appeared to dangle and lack good contact with her horse. As Morien watched Iso, she could see all sorts of small tensions and distortions in her body that prevented Charlie from performing well although overall he managed to appear competent. She wondered if she dared make a comment when Iso rode over despondently.

"He just doesn't seem to understand and is almost reluctant at times."

"He appears to me to have a lot of talent. May I have a sit on him?" Morien asked.

"Of course," said Iso slipping out of the saddle and giving Morien a leg-up.

Morien walked Charlie around for a few minutes on a loose rein allowing him to stretch the tense muscles. Then she brought him to hand and started to ask questions. At first Charlie was hesitant, waiting for the strong leg aids that Iso used. Then he cottoned on to the slight weight shifts, lightened and began to flow. Morien took him through his whole repertoire, exploring his capabilities just, she realised, as Drago had explored Merlin's paces. *I wonder what he'd think if he could see me now. The little flirt showing off, I suppose,* fleeting pain touching her abdomen. Then she became so absorbed that she forgot about Iso who was watching dumbstruck. Charlie was so light and responsive floating sideways with the correct bend and lengthening effortlessly. He just danced under her through every pace until she asked for walk and made a great fuss of him as they joined Iso.

"A really nice horse," she said

"What on earth did you do to him?" Iso was so amazed. "He looked so happy and relaxed. Are you a witch?"

"No, no," laughed Morien "I suppose I just use a different style which is all about weight shifts. He soon understood."

"Teach me," demanded Iso. "I always knew Charlie had it in him, but we never seem to win. Now I see that his problem must be me."

And so, it was that Iso remounted. Morien took her right back to basics on the buckle end of the reins, explaining about weight and containment rather than kicking and cranking in the front end. Iso was a quick study and Charlie began to go really well for her.

"What a revelation. Why have I never come across this before?"

At lunch in the farmhouse with her father she positively glowed. "Dad, do you know that today on the road you found gold dust?" She raved on so much about Morien's skill with Charlie that Morien ended up blushing.

"To think that I've been riding all these years and didn't understand all the subtleties." Iso explained to her father about Morien's background in the circus.

"I always thought circuses were cruel," said Iso's father. Morien squirmed in her seat, remembering Drago yet again and all his prejudices.

"I really can't understand how we managed to get such a bad reputation," commented Morien. "I know there are bad trainers, but they also exist outside the circus so to label us as the worst simply isn't fair."

"I suppose it's the treatment of the wild animals that upsets most people. They prefer nowadays to see them running free in their natural habitat. Even zoos are coming under scrutiny."

"Yes, I can understand that, but just because they are in a circus doesn't mean they are ill-treated. In fact, quite the reverse. The keepers often make absolute fools of themselves, treating their charges like babies." Morien reminisced.

The discussion was broken up by the arrival of the farrier. He examined Merlin's hoof and removed the shoe.

"There's a bit of bruising here which needs to clear up before he's re-shod. It shouldn't take more than a few days. Cut his food and just light walking exercise or turn him out during the day. Give me a ring at the end of the week and I'll come back." As he and Iso chatted near the van, Morien's heart sank. What would Iso think of her uninvited guests. Would she let them stay? At least the farmhouse looked big enough to have a guest room.

"Well, your loss is my gain," Iso joined her "although I suppose it's spoiled your holiday." she pouted. "But you simply have to stay here and help me until Merlin's better."

"Are you sure?" queried Morien. "After all you don't know me."

"I know a good thing when I see one," retorted Iso. "Anyway, you could hardly run off with the family silver, on horseback with your small rucksack, even if we had any." After all her previous treatment, Morien was over the moon. Taking her silence as a negative Iso said.

"I could, of course, drive you back home, but please say you'll stay till the end of your holiday."

Having nowhere to go left Morien with no alternative. Here she would be hidden from prying eyes and Drago would have no way of finding her. As she thought of him, her heart raced in a mixture of fear and desire.

"I'd simply love to stay and help you. I can pay for my keep," she said.

"Great," said Iso "Let's turn Merlin out in the paddock for some air to stretch his legs 'cos I've two more horses to exercise before tonight.

"I don't think that's a good idea," Morien paused. "He's a stallion."

Iso looked momentarily dismayed. "That's difficult," she said. I don't think our fences are high enough to keep him in if he gets wind of a mare."

"Never mind. I'll loose school him in the manege later. Although, he's had lots of exercise already today."

They spent the afternoon on the cross-country course with Iso's horses, Charlie and Gazelle. To Morien, the non-jumper, the fences looked enormous and truly horrible. There was no way she was going to attempt them, so she left the jumping to Iso, who obviously loved it all. She was happy to sit on Gazelle while Iso worked Charlie. From time to time they changed mounts so that Iso could put each horse at the different problem fences.

"If you can stay till the weekend," said Iso as they rode back "you could come to Tweseldown with me as my coach. I really would appreciate your help."

"Why not," said Morien "I'm a free agent."

Back at the farmhouse they found Iso's father reading the local paper. He turned the pages and laid it on the table to reveal a picture of Morien on Merlin receiving her rosette for the Kür, under the headline "Unknown rider takes top prize at international competition". Two pairs of accusing eyes turned on Morien. The caption under the picture read "Grey stallion missing from Wilton Hall." All Morien's hopes of seclusion and anonymity faded. The photo was so clearly her. Her dressage knowledge was totally revealed making her circus story sound like subterfuge and lies. How could she explain? Morien was incensed. It all made her seem like a common criminal.

"Merlin really does belong to me," she said simply. "They have no right to do this to me."

"How do we know that?" demanded Iso's father. All your talk of the circus could simply by fairy stories." He scowled. Now I know why we're always glad when the circuses move on. You lot obviously can't be trusted."

Morien felt humiliated. Did the Baron's fingers stretch everywhere? Would she never be free? It now seemed to her that every time she found some security and happiness, some gremlin came and pulled the rug out from under her.

"The circus story is true," she said "They know about it at Wilton Hall. The Earl used to be in the circus and knew my father."

Iso's father was clearly annoyed and feeling he'd been duped. "A likely story, I'll have to 'phone the police."

"Just a moment dad." Iso was torn between the two. "Phone Wilton Hall first and ask a simple question – who owns the missing horse?" Her father looked dubious.

"It's only fair," said Iso. "If Morien's telling the truth, then she has every right to do as she pleases." Morien felt cold with fear as he went to find the 'phone book. "And don't tell them who you are." she added as he dialled the number. "Because Helen is a friend of mine, and we don't want them to know where Morien is at the moment."

What would they say? Morien was apprehensive. The Baron was obviously intent on getting her back – or at least the horse. What a hypocrite!!

"Yes, I want to know about this missing stallion. Has he been stolen? ....no? Thank you." He turned to the girls "No, he hasn't been stolen. They just want to locate him. Why?" he looked sternly at Morien.

"It's a long story," sighed Morien.

"We've got all evening," he said coldly. Slowly and painfully Morien started from the beginning, from the death of her father to the win at the Kür and the pregnant mare. She glossed somewhat over her relationship with Nathan and his son.

"I can't go back," she murmured "I'm such a Jonah that I was almost afraid to go near the Baron's horses. I just couldn't prove that none of the catastrophes were my fault."

"Why didn't you go back to the circus, if that's really where you came from?"

Iso came and put her arms around Morien as the tightly controlled tears started to flow.

"I would not have been welcome. They have another act now taking my father's place. Anyway, there was no way I could be anywhere near Gino."

"Well, it's all a bit far-fetched," said Iso's father "and, if it's lies, we can easily find out. You can stay here as planned until your horse is fit, while I do some detective work. I'm not so callous as to throw out a lame horse, but I'll be watching you"

"Please don't give me away," begged Morien "I'll go as soon as Merlin is shod."

"Well, I believe her," championed Iso. "I've seen her work a horse. And that man's a fool if he didn't realise your talents." she made a noise of disgust.

On her own upstairs Morien reflected that once again she was surrounded by uncertainty. If they threw her out now, what could she do? She sat hugging herself as memories of her father flooded over her. Truly she was still grieving. Was it only three months since he went?

Then she remembered the cufflinks and rummaged around in the bottom of her rucksack. She was pretty sure they were gold. Looking more closely at the engraving she wondered if it was some sort of crest with its two rearing horses. They must be worth something, she thought. But no matter how dire her straits, she would never sell them. Dry eyed she rocked gently back and forth keening quietly as the pain overwhelmed her For a long time haunted by her insecurity, she let her grief take control.

CHAPTER 26

The next few days there was an uneasy peace with Iso's father. Iso and Morien worked with Iso's horses. She was taking Charlie and Gazelle to Tweseldown on the weekend as planned.

"So much depends on the dressage marks nowadays," sighed Iso "especially as there are so many reliable jumpers. They can't make the cross-country courses much more difficult for safety reasons."

Morien studied the dressage tests and explained to Iso what the judges were looking for and how to balance her horses through the more difficult combinations.

"If you draw the test out on a piece of paper, you will see the patterns you have to create," she explained, "If the test is well constructed it becomes clear that certain shapes and movements are linked to one another to enable the best response." Iso looked mystified.

"Here, for example. This tight 10 metre circle in the corner gets your horse's hocks well under him and concentrates his powerful energy. This is followed by a lengthened trot across the diagonal. Get the first circle right and the second movement just happens, provided, of course, that you hold the energy in your hand. Let's take Gazelle out in the manege and have a try."

Iso struggled to understand as guided by Morien she followed her instructions. The improvement was remarkable. For the first time in her life, Iso actually understood the mysteries of the dressage phase.

The farrier had 'phoned to say he had to cancel his visit until after the weekend. Iso was secretly pleased as Morien was able to go to the competitions with her.

They were at the venue really early on the Saturday. The show site at Robertsbridge was very different from Morien's previous encounters – again a hive of activity. Morien was on edge. She knew she was being silly, but she kept expecting the Baron to pop up from nowhere and her heart kept jumping whenever a lookalike materialised near her.

Iso explained that they had to inspect the courses, cross-country and show jumping to assess the difficulty and find the best line to ride. Leaving the horses safely munching hay in the horse box they set off for the cross-country course.

"You're so brave," said Morien standing at the edge of a brook spanned by a massive fence made from telegraph poles which seemed taller than she was.

"I'm not brave. I just love it, the thrill. It's exhilarating." Her eyes sparkled as she paced out the distances for take-off.

The course was just under four miles in toto. They walked it three times – once just to look, twice to assess all the different approaches and thirdly, to decide the final route and commit it to memory.

"Phew", said Morien laughing "I'm worn out and the competition hasn't even started."

"Well, you can see how important it was. Come on. We've still got to walk the show-jumping."

"And the dressage arenas," said Morien

"What?"

"Oh yes. It could make all the difference." Morien insisted which was all new to Iso. Morien explained the importance of level ground and odd depressions which could spoil a horse's rhythm if not anticipated.

By the time they had finished the secretary's tent was open, so they registered and then went for a quick snack of coffee and bun. "I feel really calm today," said Iso "you seem to inspire so much confidence."

"Good, that's exactly how you should feel After all it should always been fun, showing off your beautiful horses. Let's go and prepare them." Morien became business like. The dressage times were fairly close, so Iso needed Morien's help with loosening up and settling the two horses. Having three events in one day meant shorter preparation time for each phase to conserve energy Morien rode Gazelle to loosen and relax her, keeping her calm and receptive so that Iso could concentrate on giving of her best on Charlie.

Morien watched Charlie's test and was pleased to see Iso had him going really freely. They only made a couple of very small mistakes. Gazelle, being a mare, was a bit more temperamental but still her test was good taking into account the overall standard. Iso was over the moon when her dressage results came through – the best ever. She was in the lead with Charlie and in 7th place with Gazelle out of a large field.

Next, they came to the cross-country phase For most of the time, Iso was out of sight. Morien held her breath for nearly the whole round. Because she had stayed near the finish, she had to rely on the loud speaker system providing a running commentary. Both horses went clear and were well within the time, so no more penalties had been incurred. Finally, it was the show jumping. The jumps looked huge, and the course complicated but Iso wasn't fazed. Charlie went clear but Gazelle had a fence down – four penalties! However, many of the other competitors did badly in the show jumping. It was really exciting because they had to wait right until the last horse had jumped before it became clear that Charlie had won. His first ever at this standard Gazelle just managed to hold onto her 7th place. Iso was covered in glory and received congratulations from every corner.

At the prize-giving Morien was transported back to her win at the Kür. In her mind's eye, she could see the Baron, so proud, sharing her glory. It had been the peak of all her happiness – success with Merlin and being in his good books. Then it had all collapsed like a house of cards.

She moved in closer to get a clearer view of Iso. Suddenly she felt someone staring at her and turned to the fixed gaze of the woman who had been looking for a horse for Sabrina at the Kür.

The fixed gaze turned to a smile of recognition, and she started to move over. Morien ducked away into the crowd hoping the connection with Iso hadn't been observed. At the horse lines, she hid amongst the lorries to ensure she hadn't been followed. Relief there was no sign of the woman. Unobtrusively she made her way to Iso's lorry. It was then that it came home to her that she was only about 30 miles from Wilton Hall and, in the country, everyone knew everyone else. Silly of her to think she could hide.

Iso returned to the lorry on a great high. "First at last," she breathed caressing Charlie.

As they were prepping the horses for travelling home a tall young man approached them. "Hey, Iso. Very well done today. I always felt you had the talent." He gave Charlie a pat.

"You mean Charlie," laughed Iso as he gave the horse a good pat. He turned.

"No actually, I mean you," was the retort. Iso went bright red and hid her face as she attended to the leg protectors on the horse. Then standing up again she said "I'd like you to meet my new coach, Morien. Morien this is Simon, Simon – Morien."

"Pleased to meet you," said Simon. "You've certainly transformed Iso's dressage marks. The horse has always been a brilliant jumper and she's a good jockey over fences. It was just the dressage holding her back." Turning to Iso he said "Well we'll be watching you Keep it up." He strolled away.

"Wow," said Iso. "That was praise indeed. He's on the British selection panel. He's actually noticed Charlie."

"I rather got the impression that it was more than just Charlie he was interested in." Morien watched Iso's face closely. She was absolutely glowing.

"Oh OK. Yes, I do fancy him. Have done for years, but it's like worshiping a god. I never thought he would so much as look at me never mind actually speak. How'd you guess?"

"You're glowing. He certainly seems a nice sort of chap and took the trouble to congratulate you. He seemed quite genuine."

Iso looked embarrassed. "You can talk," she said. "You ought to see your face when you talk about the Baron."

"Don't be silly," said Morien loading the last horse on the lorry.

Once the ramp was closed, they chatted as they drove home.

"Well, you do fancy the Baron don't you. If you didn't care, why are you so cautious about meeting him again."

"Well ….," said Morien "I don't understand my reactions to him. He seems to mesmerise me like a rabbit in a spotlight, leaving me helpless."

"That's the chemistry of attraction," laughed Iso "Surely you've felt that magnetism before with the lads."

"There plenty of eligible ones around, I suppose, but they never had any effect on me like he does. It was so bad at Wilton Hall that I found my whole day revolving around him, even when he was really mad at me. Do you think he has that effect on all women?"

"Well, he certainly is a magnet. At the last Hunt Ball, he was surrounded by every eligible woman in the room."

"I bet he loved it."

"I'm not sure that he did. He hardly asked anyone to dance and then only the safe matrons. He went home early too."

"I don't believe you. The way he behaves when I am around makes me think he's an utter rake, out any bit of skirt. He's like a stallion when the mare is on heat, can't wait to get on with it."

"Then from what I've seen and heard, that's completely out of character."

"Then he must be a secret Lothario."

"Honestly, Morien, for someone who is so intelligent and wise with horses with people you are so naïve. It's now so obvious to me that you're both in love."

"Ridiculous!" Morien retorted.

"I can see he's got you hook line and sinker."

"That's not fair."

"Well, that's attraction for you."

"Is that how you feel when you see Simon?"

"I must say I've had a crush on Simon for months."

"I hope he likes you too then. You deserve someone like him. He's nice and into horses too."

"So do I," murmured Iso as she drove the lorry in through the farm gates.

Iso's father was as delighted as she was when he heard of the day's exploits and duly admired the red rosette.

"Well, I've also been busy," said Dad. The girls looked at him expectantly.

"I found Renaldo. The circus is still in the area, at Arundel. From what you said I realised that it couldn't be too far away, so I made a few enquiries," he said simply. Morien melted inside with relief. "He confirmed your story, right down to the sabotage."

"You're a genius, Dad," said Iso.

"He also said that the Earl had been to see him, thinking you had returned to the circus."

"I feel really bad leaving both of them without a word, but I felt it better that no one should be compromised by knowing where I was. Anyway, there was no way I was going back to Gino."

"Well, you can continue to stay here with a clear conscience, especially since Iso is benefitting so much from your tuition," said Iso's father "I've told Renaldo that you are safe with us,"

"Thank you thank you so much." Morien was so relieved.

"Renaldo also said the Baron is very upset at your disappearance."

"Spoilt his breeding programme, "said Morien scornfully trying to control the sudden beating of her heart.

"Could be," said Dad quizzically. Morien could feel the query in his mind and wondered what else Renaldo had said as she saw the beginnings of a smile on Iso's face.

"Anyway, with luck he won't find me if no one gives me away." Morien hoped the woman at the showground hadn't recognised her.

CHAPTER 27

As they settled for supper Iso's win became the main topic. "I have been trying so hard for so long that I truly believed I needed better horses," said Iso "It just goes to show what a little understanding can do." She smiled at Morien.

"And guess what, Dad, that guy Simon who looks after the British teams, you know the one who helped us when we first bought horses all those years ago, well, he came over specially to congratulate me and Charlie. Said he'd be watching me."

"So, is all your hard work coming to fruition? You certainly deserve it for perseverance."

"Let's see," said Iso.

The telephone rang and Iso's father answered it. He turned and held out the 'phone to Morien. "Since he seems to have found you, I think you'd better take this all." Morien turned white.

With great reluctance Morien took the handset.

"How did you find me?" she asked

"Many friends in many places. Local radio and papers are a good network."

"How dare you advertise for me like a common criminal." She suddenly raged at him, walking out into the corridor.

"How else could I find you when you had simply evaporated? Actually, it was the farrier who told us. He didn't know you were hiding."

"Why the importance, I was only a lowly working pupil."

"Ah yes, but one with a lot of talent and a very talented horse. Please come back."

"You mean, please bring Merlin back."

"No, my father misses you and we really do want you back."

"What," expostulated Morien. "I think my absence is a lot less worrisome than my presence. You're safer without me. You should have been delighted to see the back of me."

"My horses certainly have not suffered since you went."

"There you are then. In your eyes, I could do nothing right."

"Well, I admit, I was angry at all the catastrophes and also shocked at the subterfuge about the circus. My worst fears forced down my throat without my knowing – the ultimate betrayal."

"Huh! All your fine theories in pieces."

"True. I was so indoctrinated that I never looked beyond my prejudices." Drago sounded chastened

"Yes, I hope you choke on them In my eyes, you're a jumped-up, self-opinionated ass," said Morien disgustedly.

"I beg your pardon," he retorted.

"Yes, never looking beyond your own prejudices or understanding the sensitivity of others. Don't you see that despite your attitude and your father's disability, he's backed you all the way. With you it's all me, me, me. I hope you now realise how you've maligned him for so many years."

There was silence so Morien kept up the attack remembering his flirtatious behaviour.

"And you have the manners of a gutter snake," she flamed and hung up on him.

The others had been pretending not to listen, but Morien knew they'd overheard.

"Well, that put him in his place. I'm going out for some fresh air."

She was totally incensed and quite red in the face, never before having been so rude to anyone. Why did he bring out the worst in her? But, looking at the stars brought back another memory – the night they'd found Iatro. Damn him, was he going to haunt her forever?

By Monday, Merlin's foot was decidedly better so the farrier was able to shoe him. Morien began to collect her things together ready to leave.

"Do you really have to go?" asked Iso "From what you've said, you've nowhere to go to anyway and we're benefitting so much from your help."

"It's not fair of me to make you party to my deception," said Morien. "I don't want you telling lots of lies on my behalf." She'd told Iso about dodging the woman at the prize giving. "I expect that's how they managed to find me I'll head on up to Helen's fiancé's place. By now they've probably contacted him and as he was totally innocent, they won't look there again." However, Iso had other ideas and persuaded her to stay on.

"That's quite silly," she said "We've got the space here. Merlin's settled in well. I've got all the facilities for training.

Why would you want to go? You haven't got a job to go to, and I need you."

"I don't want you to get into bad odour with your neighbours," protested Morien.

"That's unlikely now, since the Baron knows where you are and anyway, what I do is my business. You can see that I'm being quite selfish in that respect, my personal success being much more important than a bit of gossip," Iso said earnestly.

"You're right I don't have anything to hide and teaching you and your horses is more like fun than work."

"Good. Then you'll stay?"

"What choice do I have?" laughed Morien.

Several weeks passed with Morien totally absorbed in teaching Iso the finer skills which brought more dressage points at every competition. Iso quickly become a star. Word spread and Iso's friends started asking for help too. This began to provide Morien with an income to pay her way. With Merlin fully recovered she worked him daily with Iso who was still mesmerised by the ability of horse and rider. Nor could she believe her luck since she was now being considered on a short list to represent Britain. However, Morien still felt she was imposing.

Life was falling into a pleasant routine and Morien enjoyed travelling with Iso and seeing her growing successes. From time to time, she phoned Nathan who, quite unashamedly, said he was missing her. He laughingly told her that Drago was a reformed character. The mare was showing her pregnancy and the foal was growing apace.

Then one evening - "There's a message for you on the answerphone from Renaldo," said Iso. "They're still at Arundel and he's asking if you can go over for an afternoon soon."

"That's strange," mused Morien

"Let's go tomorrow." said Iso excitedly

"OK. There's probably a matinee."

As it happened, they'd overlooked the distance and were late, but they still managed to get some tickets and sneak in. Iso was enthralled and Morien was longing for Renaldo's act with all its good laughs. But, he didn't appear. Morien knew straight away, despite the costumes that the clown wasn't Renaldo.

As the performance ended, she rushed Iso out and along the living lines to Renaldo's van. She knocked and entered without waiting. Renaldo was lying on his bunk looking quite grey with apparent pain.

"Renaldo, what's happened?" Morien cried. He managed a strained smile.

"Good to see you, little one. Done something to my shoulder." Morien knelt down beside him and took his hand, while Iso hovered uncertainly in the doorway.

"This is my friend, Iso who's letting me stay with her at present." Renaldo raised a tired hand.

"Ah yes. I spoke with her father. Excuse me, not getting up." he said wryly

"What happened?" demanded Morien

"Fell awkwardly in that tumbling routine and hit the boards," he said ruefully

"Have you seen a doctor?"

"No point. We have to move on tonight. Must do my bit."

"You'll do no such thing," exclaimed Morien. "I'm taking you to the hospital straight away." She refused to be deflected and Iso agreed with her.

"Looks nasty to me." she said eyeing his grey features. Morien turned to her

"If you could just give me a hand to unhitch the truck from the trailer, I can take Renaldo to the hospital in the truck. It will leave you free to get home."

"Sure, you can manage alone?"

"Yes, if you don't mind feeding Merlin for me."

"OK"

"It may take hours at the hospital, so I'll stay with Renaldo overnight and 'phone you in the morning."

"Here, you'd better take my mobile in case you can't find a phone. Let me know what happens. Oh, and I can come and fetch you if you need it."

"Thanks a million."

Together they released the truck and then helped a protesting Renaldo into the front seat. Morien locked up and climbed into the driving seat.

"See you later," called Iso going to her car.

When Morien and Renaldo reached the hospital, they were greeted with a long wait. People came and went. Forms were filled in and life histories taken. After nearly four hours, they ended up in the X-ray department. The eventual diagnosis was a dislocated shoulder and suspected hairline fractures to the ribs.

The doctor put the shoulder back explaining that the only treatment was rest and nothing strenuous to allow the muscles to mend and the ribs to knit. He arranged the arm in a sling.

"No strapping nowadays and no driving for at least a week," he said writing out a prescription for pain killers. "Take these now to help the pain."

"I'm glad I made you come," said Morien feeling her actions had been justified. "You couldn't possibly have travelled with your shoulder out."

It was about midnight when they got back to the circus field As they turned in through the gate Morien gasped. Of the circus, there was no sign. Just one lone caravan sitting forlornly in solitary isolation, some ruts and flattened grass being the only evidence of earlier occupation. Morien was stunned. She had forgotten the circus was due to move on. Surely someone would have waited to help Renaldo. Renaldo, who had been sleeping, sensed her shock. She was devastated.

"What is it?" he asked sleepily

"They've gone without you," she cried. He looked out for the first time, his face becoming more dawn as he took in the scene.

"Well, I couldn't expect the whole outfit to wait for me," he joked feebly.

"But someone should have stayed to help you," said Morien indignantly. "Maybe there's someone in your van." She helped Renaldo out of the truck and went to the locked door. Of course, no one was there. She had the key. She unlocked and let them in.

There was an envelope taped to the door. She removed it and passed it to Renaldo to read as she prepared some tea. Probably details of the next venue, she thought. Renaldo's startled gasp brought her to his side.

"What is it?"

"Our friend, Gino," sighed Renaldo "has just dispensed with my services." he handed her the letter.

"What? How could he do this to you when you are injured?" She moved to the light to read the letter.

"'You know we can't afford to carry any passengers,'" she read "'Dismantling tonight short-handed was a nuisance. Enclosed are three weeks' wages in lieu of notice I'm sure your little girl will take care of you.' Of all the cheek!" Morien was incensed "After all your years of loyalty, digging him out of catastrophe after catastrophe. How could he?"

"He never really forgave me for helping you. He'd set his heart on your virginity and we thwarted him."

"It didn't merit this kind of spite," she said sadly. She sat on his bunk and put her arm around him.

"Let's get you down to sleep and we'll work something out in the morning."

CHAPTER 28

Renaldo needed no rocking. The pain and the shock had taken their toll and Morien realised for the first time as she loosened his clothing that he was physically an old man. She'd never really taken this in before.

She found herself a blanket and bedded down on the spare bunk. Sleep escaped her as she dwelt on the injustice of it all. What on earth could they do? She was already imposing on Iso and her father so she could hardly land them with another mouth to feed. She knew Iso's father would help out temporarily but what of the long term?

Renaldo groaned in his sleep. Poor man. She tried to imagine how he must feel, tossed out on the scrap heap like a piece of garbage from the only life and group of friends he had. Totally bereft.

She tossed and turned the night away. There has to be a solution. Perhaps Derek could use him as a caretaker or something.

As exhaustion began to overtake her, but she still couldn't sleep. She fingered her father's photo album that Renaldo had left on the table for her to take away. It fell open. Morien studied the pictures. She realised that it was her father's history, almost like a diary. There were pictures of a large house with horses and riders on the drive. There was a wedding photo – was that her mother? She looked closely. The bridegroom was definitely a younger version of her father. There were other pictures of a stable block and of individual horses, all replicas of Merlin.

Then she came to a blank page. The next page showed a photo of a burning building. It seemed to be quite an inferno. This was followed by pictures of the circus. She could see a younger Renaldo. Some photos were of a little girl and then of a teenager. She could just remember those being taken. Something dropped onto the floor. She bent down to pick up her father's passport that she had stuck in the album at the last moment when leaving the trailer.

She flicked it open. Count Pavo Castini Demirović she read. Was this his? But wait a moment – the photo was of a young him. The country of origin was Croatia and the place of birth

159

was given as Varazdin. This couldn't be real. She hugged it to her. What if it was She searched her memory.

Then she opened the bulky envelope accompanying the album and took out the documents. There she found her birth certificate – Morien Castini Demirović born in Varazdin. There was also her father's marriage certificate. She opened another sheet. It was a claim for asylum in Britain together with an acceptance certificate and another for British citizenship. So, she was born in Croatia and never knew. At last, she had an identity.

Lying on the table next to the box of albums was the military suit belonging to her father. It now rang bells in her mind which she couldn't place.

Then she remembered the cufflinks and rummaged around in the bottom of her rucksack. She was pretty sure they were gold. Looking more closely at the engraving she wondered if it was some sort of crest with its two rearing horses. They must be worth something, she thought. But no matter how dire her straits, she would never sell them.

As she fell eventually fell asleep, she tried to recall any moments in her life with her father that indicated this background. But it was all a blank. When she had tried to talk about their past to find out about her mother, her father had just clammed up and she thought this was because he'd never recovered from losing his wife.

The light was filtering through as Renaldo began to wake. Fortunately, they still had some fresh water in containers, so Morien put the kettle on then splashed her face in the tiny bathroom before taking him some tea and pain killers.

"How are you feeling today?" she asked helping him to sit up.

"Mauled, I think would be a good description." There was a knock on the van door. Morien opened it to a bright faced farmer. "Will you be moving soon? I need to let my stock back into this field shortly."

"Tell him "Yes"" called Renaldo "About an hour, if he can wait that long."

"OK." was the response "but no longer as I've got to go to the market sales today." He loped off whistling.

"We've got to work out what to do," said Morien trying to be practical. "I expect Iso's father would let you stay until your shoulder's better. Then what?"

160

"Let's get some breakfast while I think." Renaldo wanted to know about all her adventures since leaving the Hall, reprimanding her lightly for not keeping in touch.

"Oh, I know that was so unkind, but I knew they would twist your arm if you knew where I was and being at Iso's was all so unexpected – a godsend really."

Their meal over and everything battened down, Morien re-hitched the truck and helped Renaldo up.

"Please will you stop at the first telephone box where there is suitable parking." requested Renaldo.

Morien was so busy manoeuvring, opening and shutting gates and concentrating on the unfamiliar vehicles that it was some time before she asked who he wanted to 'phone.

"Why, Nathan, the Earl, of course," he smiled

"Oh."

"We've always had an understanding and when we last met, he invited me to move in there when I retired. I didn't expect it would be so soon."

"Of course, of course," said Morien hiding the surge of emotion this prospect brought to her. What if the Baron answered the 'phone? Could she cope if she heard his voice Morien remained quiet until they found a suitable phone box and pulled up, her stomach churning at the thought of returning to Wilton Hall. Would he be there? Would they meet?

Renaldo handed her some coins. "I need you to make the call," he said knowing that it was going to be difficult for her. "I don't think I can keep climbing in and out of the truck. Will you do this for me?" Morien smiled her assent, so choked that she was unable to speak.

In the shelter of the kiosk, she stood gazing at the phone feeling that the receiver would burn if she picked it up. Dragging her mind back to the job in hand "This won't do," she chastised herself. It was then that she remembered Iso had given her her mobile, which was still in her pocket. Taking a deep breath, she dialled the number. It took only a brief moment to get through. Helen answered. She was overjoyed to speak to Morien

"I hope you are going to tell me you are coming back."

"Well er.."

"Derek and I have set the date and so far, we can't find anyone as good as you to do my job."

161

"Oh Helen. You know I'm helping Iso and she's making a breakthrough."

"Well, you could still do that from here." Morien made a non-committal sound.

"Please…"

"Look I need to speak to the Earl. I've got a bit of an emergency."

"You're not hurt, are you?"

"No, no just need a word."

"OK, I'll put you through, but you will think about it, won't you?" There were some clicks and a ringing tone. Then Rankin answered. He recognised her at once.

"May I speak to the Earl?"

"Oh, Morien, is that really you? We do miss you."

"Yes"

"I'll put him on."

"Thanks." There was a pause.

"He's just coming."

"Morien! To what do I owe this pleasure?"

"Renaldo," she said flatly. "He hurt his shoulder and Gino has sacked him and deserted him."

"What!" expostulated the Earl

"He's totally alone and in lots of pain. Can I bring him over to you?"

"Of course, there was no need to ask. Come at once."

"Oh, thank you. He'll be so relieved." Morien then dialled Iso's number.

"You, OK?" asked Iso

"Yes. Renaldo had a dislocated shoulder and broken ribs," explained Morien

"Very painful," responded Iso "Good thing we went over."

"You can't imagine what's happened now. The circus departed and just left his trailer in the field. Renaldo was shattered although he made a good job of hiding it."

"What? I don't believe you. I can't believe anyone could be so callous," exclaimed Iso "Bring him over here at once."

"Well, as you know, he's an old friend of the Earl I've just 'phoned and I'm taking him down to Wilton Hall now. I just wondered if you would have time to come and pick me up, say, in a couple of hours. I don't want to hang around. I'm definitely persona non grata."

"OK, I get the picture. I wanted to see Helen anyway. I believe she's setting the date."

"You're right," said Morien returned to the truck.

"We're on our way," she said. Renaldo's relief was palpable.

CHAPTER 29

The roads were reasonably clear, so they made good time. All through the journey Morien's fear of an encounter with the Baron increased. She began to feel sick. In her mind's eye, she could see him outside the house waiting for her to drive up. Then the image changed to the stables, and she could see him striding down to the indoor school. There was, in reality, no way in without the possibility of a meeting. To distract herself she chatted with Renaldo. Also she wanted to take his mind off the pain he was feeling.

"How did you come to meet my father?" she asked.

"Ah, now there's a story. It was back in the '90s"

"Tell me," she asked.

"Well, back when you were little, Gino's father was in charge of the circus, and we used to have three months each year in Europe. Great fun travelling all over the place. That particular year we were over near the Austrian border with Slovenia. It was the time of the Croatian War of Independence and there were many refugees crossing through."

"It must be ghastly to be a refugee with nothing but what you stand up in."

"Well, that's just what you were. Your father, brought you to the circus to cheer you up. You must have been about three years old – quite a cheeky miss," he laughed recalling the incident. "It seems you were so taken with the clowns that Pavo had to bring you around the back to find us. We got talking. He told me the Serbs were bent on ethnic cleansing, rounding up all his friends and neighbours requisitioning their properties, leaving them homeless. His stud farm was next.

Then the bombing started. As the bombing got closer to his property, he bundled his valuable horses into the horsebox with you up front and headed for the border. I gathered that the horses were a rather special. As he drove away bombs were dropping all around. The last he saw of his home it was up in flames. Lucky to get across if you ask me."

"Gosh, poor old Dad."

"Anyway, while we were chatting I suggested that, for the time being, a good way to make ends meet for him and his horses

164

would be to join the circus. He was thrilled. Together we found Gino's father and the rest is history."

Morien wondered why her father had never told her. "I didn't know any of this," she said. "When I asked him about his family he always said 'we are travellers'. I took that to mean circus people."

"It's a strange thing but those who have suffered in war rarely talk of it afterwards." He paused. "I really miss old Pavo."

They travelled in silence for a while, each lost in their own thoughts, until Morien suddenly became aware that they had arrived. As they drove through the impressive gates onto the Estate grounds, her mind flashed back to that day when she had had her first glimpse of them. Was it really only a few months back? It felt like a lifetime.

She realised that she could hardly park in front of the house with a circus trailer, so she drove around to the horse box lines and backed the trailer in a convenient space between two lorries, where the garish signs wouldn't be so visible. She prayed that Drago wouldn't be about and found her stomach continued the familiar churning. She could no longer tell if it was hope or fear? Surprisingly, Gill appeared and came over enquiringly. Her face burst into great smiles of welcome and as Morien jumped down, she was greeted with a big hug.

"Wow am I glad to see you," exclaimed Gill. "It's been lonely without you."

"What a welcome."

"Nina didn't come back. The Baron's been moping ever since. Helen wants to leave."

"Hey, slow down," laughed Morien "and help me unhitch the trailer. I've got an injured friend in the cab."

Consternation swept over Gill as she rushed to help, eyes flashing over the sign written trailer. Then Morien introduced Renaldo.

"He's a very old friend of me and my father and also of the Earl," she explained. Renaldo's strained smile caused her to add "Got to get him up to the house." She climbed back into the driver's seat and headed off leaving a bemused Gill.

Rankin must have been on the lookout since he was down the steps waiting as they pulled up. "You remember Rankin, don't you?" said Morien as they help Renaldo out and Rankin supported him up the steps. Nathan was waiting at the door.

"Welcome, my friend," he cried "I'm so delighted you felt you could come."

"Nathan, you're as good as your promise. Quite frankly, without you, I don't know what I could have done?"

"What are friends for?" Nathan responded.

"When I hurt my back I couldn't do the heavy work properly, the setting up and taking down. All my tumbling work in my routine became really difficult and, in the end, I took that bad fall and my shoulder came out under all the strain." Nathan nodded with understanding.

"I knew the writing was on the wall. Gino simply doesn't carry dead wood," Renaldo continued "so I was simply kicked out while we were at the hospital, totally deserted. No notice, nothing for years of loyalty. Thank goodness Morien was there. If it hadn't been for her and your long-standing offer, I would still be lying in that field."

"Don't think you've come here to retire though," laughed the Earl. Renaldo raised his eyebrows. "As soon as you're mended there's work to be done."

"Good," said Renaldo knowing that his friend didn't want him to feel obligated.

"Rankin has a room ready for you. Go with him now," said Nathan all solicitous as he noticed the sigh of pain. "I can see you need rest."

"So, young lady, we meet again. Why did you run out on us?"

"I think you know." shrugged Morien

"Drago?"

"Yes. He was so angry that he'd been duped. How could I stay?"

"It would have resolved itself, given time."

"Would it, with my disastrous reputation for horse care? I bet there's been no trouble since I left."

"True, "confirmed Nathan "but Drago's been like a lost child."

"Deprived of his toys." Nathan looked at her enquiringly. "Yes, the horse to win the Kür and his breeding programme spoiled. Oh, and I hear, his girlfriend."

"You're right there. I think there was a misunderstanding there too." Nathan smiled enigmatically. "Drago can be quite

166

devious to get what he wants and although he'd dated Nina, there never seemed to be any serious intention as far as I am aware." Morien wanted to know more but he turned away to answer the demands of the telephone. "Yes, all right. That was Helen. Your friend is here to take you back."

Morien stood up. "Well, I'd better be going. Thank you so much for taking Renaldo in." She hugged him and hurried out.

As she headed for the yard, she realised that she had been on tenterhooks that the Baron would appear. Like a taut string she'd felt wired to pick up his vibrations. As it was, he hadn't come. She didn't know if she was glad or sorry. Iso was chatting away with Helen when she arrived.

"I've been trying to persuade Iso to part up with you," smiled Helen. "You've certainly created an impression."

Iso pouted slightly. "It's up to Morien."

"You've set a date with Derek, Gill says?" said Morien changing the subject.

"Yes, 10th September at my home in Lewes. I do hope you'll both come."

"Try and keep us away." Both girls laughed.

On the journey home, having assured herself that Renaldo was OK, Iso was full of Helen's impending marriage.

"It'll be fun to dress up for a change. Helen knows so many people locally, it should be quite a do."

"I've never been to a church wedding," commented Morien. "Travelling people have all sorts of different ideas, never long enough anywhere to conform. A preacher usually came to us."

"It's so strange to find you've lived such a different life from the rest of us. I've never appreciated the problems before."

"I'm learning the new ways," laughed Morien.

"Will you go back to Wilton Hall. Helen's getting pretty desperate you know and speaks very highly of you. No one she's interviewed seems at all suitable and she certainly doesn't want to stay after she's married."

"You're as bad as the rest," snorted Morien. "You know why I can't go back."

"First Nina and then the Baron?"

"Yes."

"Well, I think you ought to get things sorted. You'll never have such an opportunity again."

167

"I know."

"Just think of it. You're fond of Nathan and now your surrogate dad is there too. You'll be visiting him I suppose, so you're bound to meet the Baron. Call a truce and go back to work."

"I'll think about it. Oh, by the way, here's your 'phone."

"Thanks. I had a 'phone call from Simon this morning. He's asked me to be on the team at the next event."

"Wow. I am so pleased for you Iso. We must get in lots of extra work before then to make sure you do really well," said Morien as they drove into Iso's place.

Later she decided to take Merlin out for a hack, not having ridden him for two days. The day was sultry and warm as she ambled the country lanes Her mind was in a turmoil. So much had happened in the last forty-eight hours.

She knew she couldn't stay with Iso forever and she had felt in the car on the way back that Iso thought she was unsettled and going to leave. Also, with Helen getting married they probably wouldn't need her at the racing yard.

Going back to Wilton Hall had so many advantages. She recalled her happy ideas about breeding and training dressage horses. "You'd like that too, Merlin, wouldn't you?" It was what his destiny should be.

In fact, it seemed right for everyone. Renaldo, whom she loved, Nathan who was so kind and liked her company, Merlin would be in the right place, the business would run well. The only sticking block was the animosity between her and the Baron. Could she deny all the positive outcomes because of her personal prejudice?

She had reached to top of a small hill with extensive views way out to sea. What were her horizons she pondered for a long while as Merlin cropped the grass?

Every time the Baron came into her mind, she felt this physical surge. What did she really think about him She recalled her previous recognition of falling for him and the fact that he was attached to the spiteful Nina. Could she work under the shadow of that girl, lording it over her? Could she suppress her mooning over the unattainable? It was all too entangled, and her mind shied away. "I'll decide tomorrow." she thought gathering up the reins and heading back.

CHAPTER 30

She and Iso talked it over that evening. "Helen said that Nina is convalescing somewhere in Europe for three months, she wouldn't be around at first if you went back."

"Does Helen think Nina will come back?"

"I got the feeling she doesn't. The Baron was more than a little angry."

"Just a lovers' tiff though."

"I don't think so. I got the impression from Helen that the whole thing was more of a business arrangement."

"I don't think Nina thought so, but I did hear some talk about buildings."

"Anyway, if they want you so badly you can set your own terms. Number one – Nina is not allowed in the yard."

Morien laughed "Dream on." she said However, she thought it worth phoning the Earl.

"I'm so betwixt and between. I ought to settle matters for your sake." accepting the phone from Iso. She was put through quite quickly.

"Yes, I'm well. How's Renaldo? Oh… I'm so glad he's on the mend."

After checking on Renaldo's wellbeing, she broached the subject of Nina trying to sound impersonal.

"How's everything in the yard Is Nina running the roost?" The Earl laughed.

"You know that she didn't like me very much," she explained "and she has such influence with the Baron."

"She won't be coming back in any capacity," he confirmed "Drago won't give me his reasons but he's absolutely adamant." Morien breathed a sigh of relief.

"I expect he's missing her though."

"Not at all. He's more concerned at losing Helen."

"I'm not surprised. She holds the place together."

"Well, something's got to be settled soon. Helen's set the date."

Impetuously, Morien made up her mind.

"If the Baron will have me, I'll take Helen's job," she said quickly. "If we stay business-like, I'm sure we can resolve our problems."

"Well, he certainly knows now that you were never my mistress so that's one misunderstanding out of the way. The others he'll have to learn to live with if you can." There seemed to be a note of satisfaction in his voice which left Morien perplexed.

"When will you come?" he asked.

"Give me a day or two," was her response. "Iso and I still have a few ideas to sort out." She hung up.

She turned to Iso. "There, it's done."

"What did he say?" asked Iso

"That Nina is totally persona non grata and will not be returning."

"You said you'd go back?"

"Yes."

"When?"

"Would a couple of days from now be alright with you?"

"Of course. But you're not to desert me completely."

"I won't. After all, you're improving so fast you soon won't need us."

"Not true You yourself have always praised the 'ground jockey' approach."

"Well, I think you have a great future with Charlie and Gazelle."

Two days later Iso and Morien had just finished a session in the indoor school and were making their way to the house for a well-earned coffee when they heard a vehicle pull up in the yard and Iso's father talking to the driver. Curiosity caused them to investigate. They were confronted by a land rover and trailer driven by Rankin and the Baron. From Morien's gasp Iso realised who it was and put a protective arm around her as the vehicle door swung open and the Baron strode over. He raised his hat to Iso and turning to Morien …

"I've come to take you home, "he said. The words surprised Morien. She had only agreed to go there to work.

"I've no home, "she said haughtily.

170

"I'm offering you one," his eyes pleaded, then finally "it goes with the job."

"Wow, he's in love with you," whispered Iso in her ear.

"Rubbish," muttered Morien.

"Ah, ah," responded Iso cautioning as she joined her perplexed father, giving him a nudge that they should move out of earshot. They joined Rankin but continued to eavesdrop.

"Why do you think I can now be trusted? I seem to have caused you nothing but trouble, although I am mystified about how the disasters occurred."

"I am actually aware that they were not your fault," said Drago

"You mean you have discovered something?" A ray of hope lit Morien's eyes "I have absolutely no alibi – no defence to offer."

"Yes I know now. That's how I came to crash the car."

"Not more disasters at my door." She looked horrified.

"Nina enlightened me ..... I'll tell you all about it later." He couldn't resist it. "Nina has left and now we have Helen on the point of leaving too. You, through your sins," he looked at her wickedly, "are the only one who has a thorough knowledge on how to run the office. Our need for your help is important."

"Sounds like an offer you can't refuse," commented Iso's father. Morien knew that in reality he would be pleased to see her go.

"What about me?" Iso looked rueful

"I haven't said I'm going yet," said Morien pretending Then she looked at Drago, her insides melted, and she knew from that moment she was lost. He was waiting, breathless, just as he had been when all those weeks ago, he had asked her permission to ride Merlin.

"Is this home for both of us, me and Merlin?" she enquired.

"Of course, why do you think I've brought the trailer? And in case you think I'm only interested in a breeding programme, let me disabuse you. I just know it will have to be both or neither." Gosh did he really say that. To ensure her composure Morien pretended to prevaricate.

"Being here with Iso I now have quite a few clients, who need me. I want to continue to help them. Will I be allowed the time?"

"You shouldn't need to ask." He held her eyes and she felt the pull and became almost tongue-tied. The pause seemed to stretch forever.

"Then, I accept," she whispered.

It seemed that everyone had been holding their breath and it rushed out with a great sigh of relief as each got what they wanted. Turning to Iso she said, "I'll still come to competitions with you and help you when I'm not working."

"Great," said Iso relieved. "Since you'll be quite close, I can always box the horses over for some advice. Also, I could have a go at your cross-country fences as a change from home, that is if I am allowed," she addressed Drago.

"Be my guest." Drago raised his hat to her. Then turning to Morien asked, "Would you be ready to come now?"

"I don't see why not. Iso and I have already talked matters through since being here was never permanent." She didn't want him to know of her intention to return that day. To her surprise, he lowered the ramp on the trailer to reveal Iatro.

"I thought it would be fun to have a day off and ride back." He smiled his devastating smile. Iso could hardly suppress her mirth. "I told you so," she murmured.

While Iatro was being unloaded and tacked up Morien rushed into the house and got all her gear together. She suddenly stopped. The moment of truth. What was she doing? Was this what she wanted? Yes, absolutely. A good job, a home for Merlin and a chance to see Drago every day. Her doubts flew away.

She rushed downstairs and out to the land rover, thrusting in her backpack for Rankin to take back. Iso had fetched Merlin and saddled him for the ride.

Morien hugged Iso and her father and vaulted onto her horse. Drago was already in the saddle. So, with many promises to stay in touch with Iso, Morien waved goodbye. "I'll ring you tomorrow."

172

CHAPTER 31

"I think I must be dreaming," she thought as the unreality swept over her.

"I thought we'd go up on the Downs. When I was a kid, I used to spend hours up here on my pony."

He seemed to know all the bridleways and Morien simply followed, up, up along the grassy paths through meadows thick with flowers and blue butterflies Riding along the ridgeway they could see the glittering sea and way inland to the North Downs.

"It's such a lovely ride and I can't remember when I last enjoyed the views."

However, the beauty of the views was lost on Morien. Her feelings were in a tangle and all her focus was on this powerful man beside her.

Suddenly he turned off the path and dismounted stumbling slightly.

"I'm sorry, I didn't ask how you are after your accident." Morien joined him as they allowed their horses to crop the grass.

"Mending well. I'd like to tell you about that." She waited

"You will recall I was giving Nina a lift." He watched carefully for some reaction, but Morien stayed still.

"She thought it was the time to stake her claim and became amorous. She seemed to have total misconceptions about why she had been given a place at Wilton Hall. Obviously, my fault, I should have realised. Needless to say, just prior to a major competition, I had other things on my mind than personal attachments - the excitement of the Kür with a horse capable of winning. Nina misinterpreted my absorption with the problems of working a new horse as interest in you and lost her temper. At first it was just spiteful remarks, gradually building up through my lack of response. Then it all came out. How she had done her best to discredit you and get you sacked. I was so shocked to see such venom. I truly had no idea that people could feel that way. Suddenly I saw the whole picture from her point of view."

"I was convinced that it was sabotage even though it was subtle and plausible," commented Morien walking over to a wooden bench "But proof was hard to come by."

"I must say I began to have suspicions that someone was getting at you the night Merlin escaped, since you were right, we did close the stable door together. But then I knew you were in the habit of giving him a goodnight kiss."

"You must have realised that there's no way I would let something so precious to me get hurt, just to spite you," said Morien passionately.

"Yes, now I fully realise that. Anyway, Nina confessed all, having realised much more succinctly than I, that it wasn't just working with an exciting horse; I was emotionally involved elsewhere." Turning his deep eyes on her expectant face, Morien looked quizzical as he went on

"Despite her revelations, I was still anxious to get to the competition and, in a last desperate attempt to get my attention, she grabbed the steering wheel, just as a dog ran out into the road. The rest is history, the car a write-off and relief that neither of us was fatally or permanently injured.

Morien's face was now a mixture of relief and concern. "I'm truly sorry, for giving the impression I didn't care about your injuries. I've never asked one word about your accident."

"Shall we say that my need for information took precedence at the time?" said Drago. "All those revelations all at once were totally mind blowing."

Taking the reins from her nerveless fingers, he hitched the two horses to the bench and took her hand.

"Can you ever forgive me for how I've treated you?" he asked as she gazed up at him. "I truly thought you were one of my father's conquests when I found you hugging him that first night. After all, we don't have many friends of the family that I don't know about, and it never crossed my mind that you could be a student – and in the house! You know now that it was a complete misunderstanding." his eyes pleaded. She turned away not sure that she could handle this.

"You didn't disabuse me," he insisted.

"I couldn't. I was in a state of shock."

"Please accept my apologies for being so rude to you. Later, it was the only way I could think of to keep my hands off you, especially since I thought you were well versed with the world. I yearned for you every day and every night. God, how I wanted you. Can you understand?"

Morien still thought she must be dreaming.

"I thought you only wanted Merlin, an office slave and a roll in the hay," she said trying to make light of the situation.

His arms crept around her waist drawing her towards him. Excitement surged.

"Up here the winds blow away the past." He held her so close that she knew he could feel the frantic beating of her heart and she let her head rest on his powerful shoulder.

"Morien, my love, never before have I been so hypnotised and, yes, obsessed by a woman. It has always been horses first with me."

"Maybe this time it's because of the 'can't have' element," smiled Morien

"No, no. It's far more than that. You've haunted my dreams, kept me awake at night."

"That was probably worry about the next disaster," was her cynical response, pulling slightly away.

"You know that's not true."

"Do I?" He gently pulled her back and held her firmly she could feel his masculinity pressing hard against her. At the eye contact she was lost. His lips found hers, tongue searching deeper and deeper until the outside world no longer existed. She never wanted to leave this space, high on the hills of her love which flowed into him, the ecstasy swirling in an abyss of emotion. When he lifted his head, she felt bereft.

"You know we love each other." His eyes smouldered

"Yes," she said simply. "I too have been mesmerised by you from the start. I think it truly sparked the night we rescued Iatro."

He hugged her to him again. "And then we had that day on the beach. After that I knew I was doomed. I was so confused, thinking of you as a hussy and yet knowing you were the only girl in the world for me. I really wanted to send you away to get some peace of mind, but my heart wouldn't let me."

"I was constantly afraid that you would. For me it seemed a love/hate situation. I lived for the moment when I'd see you and then was terrified you'd find fault and throw me out."

"What a totally silly mess we've been in. My father has a lot to answer for."

"But you would never have let me come if you'd known the truth." said Morien "and we'd never have met. I think his subterfuge was worth every moment." They hugged again.

"Now that all the confusion is out of the way, I'll tell you the real reason that I brought you up here." She waited breath suspended.

"Will you marry me?" he asked simply. She must be dreaming but, as the silence lengthened her doubts evaporated like her resistance. She smiled into his eyes. This really was a dream.

"Oh yes." She melted into his kiss, enthralled by his masculine closeness. It was some minutes before they became aware that the horses were becoming restless and stamping around.

"Good old Merlin, rescuing you again," he laughed

"Merlin, you shall be the first to know," said Morien releasing the reins. "Drago and I are going to be married." The big horse nuzzled her snuffling for carrots. Surprise, surprise, Drago had some in his pocket feeding the titbits to both horses.

"I need to tell you something about Merlin now that we will be a family."

"Not more secrets I hope."

"No definitely no more secrets. Many years ago my father had a stud in Croatia breeding Lipizzaner."

"What?"

"Lippizaners. He lost everything during the war of Independence, becoming a refugee. He managed to cross the border with some of his best horses – and me. At that time, the circus was in town, and he realised that, if they would take him, it would provide a livelihood for him and his charges. Eventually they arrived in Britain."

"That was enterprise, when faced with such a catastrophe," said Drago

"Travelling as we did enabled him to locate the few resident Lippies in this country. Over a period of years, he bought a stallion and two mares from which he bred a number of foals. They were all Siglawys." The Baron gasped – these were amongst the most exclusive dressage horses in the world. "We had a liberty string of six with Merlin being trained to join it and earn his keep. Until you showed me that video of the Spanish

Riding School, I had no idea of the importance of Lippizaners and was quite taken aback. They were such friendly, co-operative horses, full members of the family."

"What I would have given to have had such a string and there they were being wasted in the circus ring."

"Never wasted," said Morien "As long as they were happy and giving pleasure to so many people, they were fulfilling their role just as well as your Viennese friends."

"I suppose you have a point."

"My father was bringing on young Merlin, who was learning well and really enjoying his work performing to the crowds."

"That would explain why he is generally so well-behaved in public. He's been brought up to it."

"Oh yes. He's certainly a show-off," commented Morien.

"Sadly, during one of their training sessions one of the lions escaped and attacked them. Merlin panicked so badly that he collided with the temporary seating. My father died instantly. In our circus Merlin became a killer and superstition would no longer allow him to be part of any performance."

"How ridiculous, " said Drago "It was obviously an accident and I'm sorry about your father. I wondered why you would never tell me anything about him when he was obviously such a brilliant horse trainer."

Morien glowed at this unexpected compliment, acknowledgement at last.

"I have Merlin's registration papers in my belongings," she said quickly. "His full name is Merlin Maestro Siglawy"

"My god today is truly my lucky day in more ways than one," murmured the Baron. "A wonderful partner and future wife, who brings as a dowry a Lipizzaner stallion. What a breeding programme we could have," his eyes sparkled as he cheekily eyed her up and down.

It was still some time before they re-mounted. They couldn't seem to get enough of each other. But eventually reason prevailed, and they made their way along the trackway and down into the valley, reaching out to touch each other whenever the path was wide enough to ride alongside.

As they rode up the drive Morien again recalled the first time, her apprehension the strangeness and immensity of it all. The stable yard still held its aura of peace, nothing had changed on the surface, but for Morien everything had changed.

"Home at last," whispered Drago "Merlin's box is waiting for him." Morien sighed with happiness. "Merlin's box" those simple words that meant belonging.

"I'll just put Iatro away and we'll go up to the house together."

Morien took Merlin to his 'home'. Everything was prepared and the minute his bridle was off, Merlin dived for the hay net. "Greedy boy," laughed Morien "Tummy first." Without turning she knew Drago was at the door. Coming in, his love reached out to her, and his arms enveloped her. "This time you don't have to push me away." he murmured.

Surfacing for air Morien did push him away. "I must put this tack away," she said.

They met Helen in the tack room She gave Morien a hug.

"Welcome back."

"You can now leave with a clear conscience," Drago told her interrupting her greetings. Helen looked mystified. "Morien has agreed to come back and take your job."

"That's fantastic. Derek will be over the moon."

"We have some other news too Morien will be here permanently – as my wife."

"That is the best news I've heard in a long time," said Helen smiling. "I always felt somehow that you two should be together instead of constantly at cross purposes. Your ideas and abilities are totally harmonious."

"We'll have to consider a double wedding," he laughed grabbing Morien's hand and heading for the house. They could see a reception party waiting for them. Their homecoming was greeted with delight all round. Iso had rung and informed everyone that the pair were on their way and of course, Rankin had returned with the trailer.

To Morien it was a moment of sheer bliss as she hugged Nathan and Renaldo.

"So glad to have you back," said the Earl, "It's really been quite dull without you."

As Morien hugged Nathan and then Renaldo, Drago called Rankin. "Break out a bottle of champagne because this is a double celebration." he requested.

"What's all this?" enquired the Earl

"Morien and I have something important to tell you both so please charge your glasses." Taking her hand, he said "Morien is not only coming back to help in the office and with the training of the advanced horses. She has also done me the honour of agreeing to become my wife."

There was a burst of delight from both Nathan and Renaldo and congratulations all round. Morien standing by the window felt such a surge of happiness as she raised her glass to the three most important men in her life – Renaldo who with his unfettered love had rescued her in her hour of need; Nathan who, against all the odds had taken her in and Drago in whose love she felt totally secure.

EPILOGUE

The wedding was the talk of the County, Wilton Hall being the most perfect backdrop for such an occasion, with horse drawn carriages for bride and groom. They had a rapturous honeymoon in Vienna where Drago took Morien to see the Spanish Riding School in its home setting. To their surprise, because he was an ex-pupil, they were invited back to meet all the team and their horses. When Morien's name was mentioned, it was discovered that her father had also been a pupil at the School, which explained his obsession with Lipizzaner.

Once home, Drago asked her to show off her other circus talents indicating that he'd always been curious about her ability to vault on such a tall horse. Morien gave a display in the indoor school with Merlin who behaved like the perfect circus horse. Thus, vaulting and leaping from the ground were introduced into the standard curriculum since Drago felt such athleticism was valuable to the students.

Morien took over the running of the office and all the business side. As Helen had predicted she was given some of the training of the young horses, her win on Merlin well remembered, making her much in demand. Thus, she had the best of both worlds. She helped Iso reach Olympic status and had the delight of seeing her win Olympic gold. Iso and Simon became an item.

Her loyal Gill went on to great successes as a show jumper which made her popular as a tutor, so she came back on the staff of Wilton Hall.

A year later the special mare had given birth to the most beautiful chestnut colt. It carried all the best attributes of its parents and in its first year was winning the in-hand classes for his age group at all the local shows. The mare was in foal to Merlin again so hopes were high for the breeding programme.

To complete their joy, Morien also became pregnant with their first child.

Lightning Source UK Ltd.
Milton Keynes UK
UKHW012035220422
401921UK00003B/222